WHITE WINTER

Roxana Vella

authorHOUSE®

AuthorHouse™ UK
1663 Liberty Drive
Bloomington, IN 47403 USA
www.authorhouse.co.uk
Phone: 0800.197.4150

Published by AuthorHouse 01/15/2018

ISBN: 978-1-5462-8708-7 (sc)
ISBN: 978-1-5462-8709-4 (hc)
ISBN: 978-1-5462-8707-0 (e)

Print information available on the last page.

DEDICATIONS

First and foremost I want to thank God for his unconditional and unfailing love.

Second I want to thank my husband for believing in me, for supporting me, and for being a constant encourager!

Maybe it was the frost that killed her. But no-one will ever really know. No-one knows about the evil that lurks beneath the white Persian carpet of snow in winter—the chill that you feel when a snowflake rests on your nose; and that sweet, warm sensation will not remain the same. It turns to the warmth of hell's hatred, and the sweetness turns to sourness. No more being cosy by the crackling fireplace as those flames are just the beginning to hell's blazing passion, its hatred of a White Winter—the missing knot in the Persian carpet of winter.

PROLOGUE

He slashed through her savagely. And blended into the icy misty air as if he was a ghost. But he wasn't … was he?

She was left there alone, trying to defeat death, but the blasts of winter swept her cold life away.

While the cheering bells echoed her last piercing scream, noone knew that the carpet of snow was now stained with intoxicated blood, the blood of the girl whom everyone loved and cherished— the same blood that will drown them in the world of the fathomless evil of the supernatural.

PART I

In the bleak mid-winter
Frosty wind made moan
Earth stood still hard as iron
Water like stone;
Snow had fallen, snow on snow
In the bleak mid-winter
Long ago

Christina Rossetti, "Mid-Winter"

THE FUNERAL

Everything seemed damp and gloomy. Everyone was in monotone. Black. What an ugly colour. Darkness. Evil. No light. No joy or peace settled in the hearts of the grieving. The sobs. The sobs were silent yet penetrative, echoing throughout the whole church, leaving a tune of melancholy and depression. Words were ministered, but nothing was heard. Nobody's ears were attentive to what was being said. Everyone was absorbed in their own memories with the deceased. Though silent, the sound of a broken heart is the loudest and most painful.

"We are all here today because Amy Saunders, at the tender age of sixteen, has left this world in an inhumane way. We pray that her soul has been saved. May the Lord lay his hands on her, and may she rest in peace. Amen."

"Amen," sobbed the congregation, oblivious to the fact that birds were chirping merrily at the windowsill as though they were messengers of encouragement and hope. Yet nobody listened to them.

But then again, nobody ever does.

Pastor Taylor had been in the ministry for a long time, but this was his first encounter with such a death. If only he had known what Amy was going through, surely he had the right tools to help her out. Her church attendance had declined recently, but every adolescent's attendance seemed to decline. He knew Amy; he was a personal friend of the family. He knew she had had her hardships, as everyone did, and she had opened up to him and his wife at times. He looked at the coffin, imagining her inside. Such a young age. What a loss. He felt …compassion for the family. This tragedy was insane.

Amy's death brought about a great state of shock and change, not just to her family, but also to her friends and neighbours. The one who was most affected by this unexpected death was Faye, Amy's eleven-year-old sister. Tom was a one-year-old, too young to understand. Besides, Tom didn't see much of Amy as she rarely spent quality time with him.

Faye loved her sister a lot—maybe too much. They shared many happy and sad memories together, and everyone was aware of their exceptionally strong, invincible bond. Wherever Amy was, there was Faye, lingering on. And wherever Faye was, surely Amy was there also. They were pleasant to be around.

Faye still could not grasp this new reality. It felt much closer to a bad dream, and she was eager to wake up soon. Her body moved towards the pulpit. Nope, she realised, this is not a dream. This is a nightmare in action. And she hated every second of it. She wrote a letter to her sister and was about to read it aloud before those present at the funeral. A knot was tightening even more in her throat as she walked towards the pulpit. All eyes were on her. Not only was the mourning aspect of it all making her emotional, but stage fright was also kicking in. All eyes were on her as small beads of sweat started to form on her forehead. Her palms were sweaty. She could feel her face flush. Could people sense she was scared to speak in front of them? She took a deep breath and forced herself to start. She looked at her paper. It was getting blurry as a mix of sweat and tears formed in her eyes. She took another deep breath and started to speak.

"Where is Amy? That was the first thing I asked my parents on that bright, sunny morning after the night when you never returned home. I actually believed that you were playing one of your tricks and would return soon. But when the sun started to set and you still hadn't returned, well, that was when I started having doubts whether you would ever come back. It pained my heart terribly, and it still does—the thought that you'd never be able to see bright sunny mornings again. Just like today, we are alive and kicking, and the sun is waiting for us to go out so that she makes us warm and gives us rosy cheeks. But you—you are in that terrible, ugly box, without air, turning even greyer by the second. The sun cannot penetrate through you to give you back life. I prayed hard to Jesus for you to return home, or at least be safe and alive somewhere out there, but he told me that you were next to him and that he's taking good care of you. I'm sure he is, but I miss you a lot.

"Your particular shrill never leaves my head.And you looked so sweet when you yelled at me whenever I borrowed one of your pencils and forgot to return it or when I borrowed your clothes without your permission. And it's a pity that your talents— especially that of acting—have died with you and that you weren't given the time to enhance them. You would have been the next big thing! I'm sure of that!

"I will never forget you. How can I? You are always treasured deep in my heart—in all our hearts. We will always carry that special place for you. You truly are a gem to us. When little Tom grows up, I promise I will tell him what a very good sister you were, but above all, what a close friend you truly were. And how special you were to everyone. I will pray for you always.Love, Faye."

Everyone was in tears. They felt sorry for Faye. It was evident that she felt miserable. Her distant eyes made people wonder if she'd ever get past this trauma. Of course, time usually heals wounds of all kinds, but does it ever patch a broken heart? Or do broken hearts carry scars until the end of time?

Faye knew more about what happened to her sister than most people thought she knew. It might not have made sense to her so far, considering the age factor and the timeless question of 'why'.

But what she did know was that her sister's death was unnatural on so many levels.

At the back of the church, Sam, Amy's ex-boyfriend, sat there, staring hard at the coffin as if he expected it to open like a jack-in-the-box and that Amy would be there, cheerful, happy, and alive. All this would have been a cruel re-enactment of some sort. Or perhaps this was a melodramatic play. He knew better. His brain tried different scenarios as a means to cope. Still, nothing worked. He was moved with compassion by Faye's letter to her sister because he knew this tragic death was partly his fault. He tried to grasp onto something in his memories that would convince him it was absolutely not his fault that Amy was dead and that he was totally innocent.But he just couldn't find anything to convince him. Besides, had he been convinced in any way, his conscience would still have haunted him throughout his entire life.He led her to it, he led her through it, and he was guilty. He felt like her blood was on his hands, even though he was not the killer.Denying it in himself, Sam still knew he could not escape what he had done. How foolish. How juvenile. Too late to be wise about it now. Just a little too late. Had it not been for his immaturity, he wouldn't be sitting there at the back, unnoticed, drenched in not just his tears but also in his guilt, pain, and remorse.

Sam was more concerned about the charges against him if he got caught rather than missing his ex-girlfriend in general. He knew more to the story than anyone else probably did. He knew everything. Yet he wasn't ready to share it all, even if his conscience begged him to do otherwise. He lay aside his conscience and thought about the blood pact he made. Sam could not back down from it now. It was way past the point of no return. And there was something else unfinished that still had to be done.

Amy was a sweet-natured girl with an extraordinary personality. Yes, she had proved to Sam that she was a very good actress as she had been utterly good at acting to her parents and family these past few months. She was good at hiding what was really going on in her life. And when she couldn't hide anymore, she tried to run away. But she got caught. She got wrapped up in an intertwined mess with no escape. Not even any hope of escape. He was cautious of the way Amy had effervesced into the acidic girl she had become. Let's just say Amy was short of luck, and no one could save her, not even when she was on the verge of changing into what she used to be once upon a time, that time when she was still with her old friends and under her parents' strict orders to return home no later than midnight. It never bothered her to be called Cinderella by her peers. But when she changed, although blessings were still around her, she could not see them. She didn't want to see. Deep down, she knew they were there, but she could not accept that something far sovereign beyond this world would still care about her, even if she started playing for the opposing team.

Amy's parents, Janice and Alfred, were crestfallen. The sweet sixteen-year-old they once had was taken from them. They couldn't bear that thought. But then, who could? How does it feel to have lost your daughter or son and to know the cause of death: murder and sacrifice? The feeling can be imagined, but the reality of it deviates far from the limited imagination of the inexperienced. The sword that cut deeply into their hearts, the sword of pain that afflicted continuous tormented wounds, was taking its toll on them. It was devastating and heartbreaking to look at the Saunderses cry their river of crystal clear pain.

Janice Saunders reminisced on the time when her daughter had come back home from school with a grin on her face that stretched from one ear all the way to the other. Janice knew something special had happened to Amy that day, but Amy had insisted that her dad had to be home, too, to tell them her great news. When Alfred returned home, Amy began talking.

"Sorry for keeping you waiting mum, but as they say, curiosity killed the cat!" she sniggered. "I hope satisfaction will bring him back!"

"No problem, dear. Just tell us what you have to say! I've been on pins and needles a long time!"

"Have you got a boyfriend?" Alfred asked her with a tone of suspicion."I bet you have! What's his name? Huh?"

"It's not a boyfriend!" said Amy impatiently.

"Come on, dear, don't be shy of us. It's very normal to date boys you know.What's his name?"

"It's not a boyfriend!"

"Good Lord, don't tell me it's a girl!" Alfred wanted to mock her. He always did when the subject turned to love and relationships.

"Alfie, dear, that was so immature of you! Our daughter's straight, and you know that!"

"Ah well, you never know, now, do you?"

"Is it a girl Amy?" asked Janice almost disgustedly.

"For cryin' out loud *no*! God, you two are so absurd and half-witted! It's got nothing to do with my love life! Gee!" And off she went to her room, stubbornly and without speaking to anyone. The parents were thunderstruck. They felt a pinch of guilt and shame for ruining her surprise to them. They still giggled.

"We have to apologize, Alfie," Janice said, still giggling silently. She tried to pull up a straight face. Oh the teenage years.

"She'll get over it … She will", he muttered.

At supper time, Amy had refused to show up in the dining room. But then she knew that if she didn't, there would be an awful lot of grumbling going on, and she just couldn't put up with that today, either. So like a dog with his tail between his legs, she went to the dining room where she found her parents waiting around the table, looking quite patient indeed.

"Hey, Amy, we're very sorry. It's just that we felt like joking with you. We hadn't thought you would take it badly the way you did. We're very sorry."

"Yeah, sure, no problem", she said with a markedly disapproving tone.

"Come on, cheer up! Bring that beautiful smile of yours to daylight again. Well, room light in this case, but do tell us your good news, please."

"Sure. Well, if you insist; excuse me for a second." Her excitement returned to her.

She showed up with a few sheets of paper and left them on the table. Suddenly she felt frozen in time, not knowing whether to read them out loud or let them read them for themselves. She thought it would be idiotic of her, so she gave them the reading role.

"Just read them." And there was no more said from Amy. Her heart started pounding and it felt as though the whole room could count every beat of her heart.

Mrs Saunders picked up the papers and started reading the essay out loud:

> "From up Here" by Amy Saunders.
> I looked down onto the world and cried a lake of cold, crystal tears. Everyone is doing it. It's as though it is a fashion—a fashion for hot, red blood. Killed. Torn apart. A nasty, brutal death. Don't they know that we're still young and defenceless?

I can't bear the sight of it. I couldn't bear the pain either. I was one of them, too. I tried to kick and I tried to scream—my silent scream. But no one heard me. In that dark warm, chamber of love, I was somehow killed. It was silver and sharp. And it passed through me. I couldn't feel my hands anymore. And I saw my feet floating. Then there was a strong wind. I didn't know what it was, but it sucked me into it, and I was terrified and in pain. I wondered where my mum was. I'm sure she would have saved me. I found myself in a huge container. It was a red sea. And I was able to see my arm and foot. But there were others, all in the same situation as I was. We couldn't understand what was happening.

When I came back up to where I originally was, I met a few of my old friends. I told them what happened to me, what I felt, what I saw. And they explained it to me.

They call it *abortion*. Up here, we call it *murder*. Many mums do it. They pay a lot of money to a doctor to kill the embryo so that mums don't give birth, and they can keep on living their lives. There are no dads involved. Just men.

I still cannot understand why they do it. How can she not love me? I was part of her. I felt comfort when I heard her pulse. I felt her breathing. What could I have done? I loved my mummy even though I never saw her face, but I could hear her speak. She had the most beautiful voice ever. I still love her and always will.

All my friends up here sometimes send letters to their mums. I sent my mum one too. I told her how much I miss her and that I'm in a safe place now. I told her that I will always love her and that I forgave her for aborting me. I told her that I called to her. Then I signed my name. "Thing", she called me. I wonder what it means. Strangely enough, all my friends are called Thing. When I sent it, I sealed it with a million kisses.

I saw her open the letter and read it. Tears filled her eyes. I wonder why. I told her I was in a safe place. I heard her say that she was sorry and never meant to hurt me. But she never hurt me. She's my mummy.

Then she sent me back a letter. She said she didn't know who or what I was. Very strange. I'm sure I sent the letter to the correct address.

It has been three years now. And I sent three letters to my mum already. She keeps telling me the same thing, but her tears keep on increasing with each letter.

But now I understand—God explained it to me. It's not fair. We lost our chance to live. We don't know what life is. And that was our priority in our existence: to experience life. I was looking forward to the day that I would be born. But that day never came.

Each year thousands of my friends called Thing join me. We're sorry for the other friends who are currently being killed the way we were.

We looked down onto the world again. We cried more cold tears. Yes, it is the fashion. Abortion. We have our motto up here, too: Lucky are those who are not aborted."

A silence filled the room, which made Amy anxious. Her mind was running with ridiculous thoughts: Did they like it? Did they hate it? They didn't say a word. Oh man, they hated it. Was it stupid? Yeah, yeah it was.

Her mind was now a canvas of confusion injected with the fear of rejection. And as with many artists, perfectionism led her to believe the most negative and critical voice she could ever hear, the one in her own head.

In reality, Amy's essay had touched everyone who read it. It had touched her lecturer's heart and obtained a top grade. It was as if Amy knew the feeling of murder, as if she had an indirect premonition of some sort because her death was similar to her essay. You could say it was retrospective irony that she'd been torn apart brutally.

Tears streamed from Janice's eyes as she reminisced. How could her little baby grow up into such a creative bombshell yet not have the time to explode into an array of opportunities? How could she get past this chapter? Was this the final chapter in her life, too? Has her life ended, too, at the death of their little beloved? She remembered the little surprise they gave to Amy to cheer her up and give her the confidence boost she needed in order to believe further in herself and her talents.

"My God, Amy, that was so beautiful and touching. You really gave me the shivers", her dad said proudly, unaware that his daughter had turned out to be such a beautiful and inspirational young lady.

"You're pretty talented, and I'm most definitely glad you are using your talent to touch hearts", her mother added as a compliment.

Both of Amy's parents had an idea of their daughter's hidden artistic talents, but they hadn't realised how well developed they had become. After their appraisal, she immediately shied away from them, wondering how she could perfect her work. Amy loved creating, but did not know how to receive criticism or appraisal. Thus at times she denied that she had ever created anything with her hands. The Saunderses knew Amy's traits. It was their idea, after all, for her to go to drama lessons. They believed that this training would build up her esteem, help her to be more confident in who she was as an individual, and to believe in herself and her talents. Drama did infact help do all of this, yet her heart still remained tender, and pride did not flourish whenever she was praised for her talents. She still blushed. And deep down she still thought that she did not deserve any attention, but her drama lessons at least taught her how to accept all of this.

She loved her drama lessons, not just because acting gave her a moral boost, but mostly because she could be whoever and whatever she wanted to be. Today she could be a fairy, tomorrow she could be a pauper. And next month—who knew? The possibilities were endless. She found she could express herself better in the shoes of other diverse characters. Her portrayals of the characters she played where always touched by a piece of her, which made the whole end product unique from her end. She was already well sought after in the major productions of her town. Others had far larger dreams for her than she did for herself.

About a month after Amy showed them her notably touching essay, Janice went up to Amy's room with a magazine in her hands.

The door was ajar, so she knocked gently. "Hey Amy, have you got a minute?"

"Yeah sure, Mum, what is it?"

She opened the door and went next to her daughter. "Is this your favourite mag?" she asked, knowing that it was so.

"Oh my God! You got the latest edition of *HotGirl*! That's awesome! I thought I had missed this edition. I had too much to do; I didn't find time to go and buy it. Gee, Mum, thanks! You really didn't have to bother. How did you know anyway that I didn't have it yet?" she asked excitedly.

"Actually, you did miss an edition. This came in the mail just now."

Amy got suspicious.

"I'm not subscribed for home deliveries though." She suspected her parents surprised her with a yearly subscription.

Her mum laughed. "Look here …"

Amy started reading and was immediately taken aback. This was simply out of the blue. She couldn't believe what she was seeing. Her essay "From up Here" was published, and she had won a cash prize for having her essay being chosen as the star story of the month! She was speechless and a little bit shy.

"Mum, you didn't have to. My God, this is great! Pinch me so that I'll know I'm wide awake. Oww, Mum! Not that hard. Oh, I can't wait to tell everyone!"

And she did. Not because it was her work being published for the first time ever but because her parents cared enough for her to show her how much they appreciated her talents. She didn't quite care whether people read her essay or not, she was just aware of how blessed she was as a person. And she prayed for her devoted parents every day, and honoured them in the best way that she knew, in the best way that she was taught. Amy was a pleasant delight, easily loveable and was never a troublemaker. They just couldn't understand what she had gotten herself into in her final months, but the end result sure wasn't what Amy or anyone else was expecting.

These thoughts were even more heartbreaking to Mrs Saunders because now she couldn't bring back Amy, and she couldn't surprise her anymore, and she couldn't watch her mature into a beautiful woman. The realization hurt too much. This was way too tough for both the Saunderses. They couldn't retain all the wonderful memories they had shared when Amy was still alive. She had slipped away.

They started to wonder if they showed enough love and care towards Amy, and if they pleased her enough. They started to believe that despite all the good things they tried to teach their daughter, they somehow failed. They felt like they failed miserably and that they were responsible for their daughter's death even though they were oblivious to everything that had truly taken place except for the aftermath. They just couldn't accept the fact that someone deliberately tempted their daughter and made use of her in such a brutal and heartless way. They couldn't adjust to the new change in their life and didn't want to readjust once more to another death.

Yes, there were other deaths before Amy. There was Holly, who died at the age of one week from heart complications. Holly had meant so much to them because after two miscarriages, Holly was a miracle—one that unfortunately didn't last long enough. When healthy Amy came along, that meant more than the world to the Saunderses. And now that healthy young girl was left to decay and wither away with her other siblings. It was just too much –like a cloud of curse hung above their heads, attracting death towards the most innocent.

Mind you, they loved Faye and Tom likewise, but Amy was always their most precious child. They claimed not to show any partiality between the girls, however obvious it still was to everyone else. They felt that Faye acted as a type of tourniquet, helping to stop the cursed bleeding from leaking anymore than it already had.

Faye had a unique character. Even though she needed a tourniquet herself to help stop her bleakness, yet she still endeavoured to support her parents and let them know that at least they still have two children who love them and care for them as much as Amy did, if not more. The Saunderses both realised that they gave way too much attention to Amy and did at times neglect

Faye, who had to watch and bear their praise and encouragement all going towards her sister rather than being shared between the both of them. She did not get particularly jealous because she could understand why. Nonetheless, she was still human, and it still hurt at times. Faye was practically an unnoticed special child because she was amazingly sensitive to the hearts of others and always sought out the needs of others before her own. But everyone took advantage of that. Faye was still immensely naive to the harsh reality of society.

The Saunderses had long been Christians, and their faith had been tested and tried in the fires so much that at times they felt it was too much of a burden, yet they kept enduring. They kept pressing forward, and kept on running this tedious obstacle race called life—trusting, praying, and serving. But now their lives crumbled, and Christ was not the centre of their lives anymore. Discreetly and without any discussion, they cast him aside like He was a rugged beggar not worth fighting for any more. They forgot all of His promises, they forgot His Word, for it slipped from their hearts. Not because it was not planted well, but because they chose to live in unforgiveness. This attitude fertilized a seed of detachment and division inside of them, and at the gush of a storm, that little rotten seed took over and started to flourish.

Faye had a strong character and kept showing respect towards her kith and kin. But deep inside, this unforeseen ordeal enervated her completely. She couldn't endure this situation that faced her. It had slapped her hard on the face. Gradually, this not only broke her and tore her apart, but it tried the patience of her closest friends, too. It had seemed that the chilled wind made its way to Faye's heart and froze it all up, leaving only an utterly narrow streak for the cold water to trickle down into the deepest chamber of her heart, that small reservoir that was filled to the rim with her love for Amy and her profound passion for classical ballet.

Sam rushed out the door just before the funeral service was over and walked steadfastly, thinking and pondering on all those faces and bare hearts.

The Saunderses were pilgrims walking on Calvary in a landscape of pain and suffering. And this stirred the sinews of Sam's heart. This massive disturbance of guilt hung like a cloud over his dusty being. Something tempted him to sweep off this dust that had accumulated on his shoulders, but the dust seemed to have coalesced onto him and wouldn't let go. This permanent burden would overrule his life. He had hastily turned into an unethical and fraudulent adolescent who topped it all off by demoralizing his girlfriend and other friends too. He was quite aware of what he had helped cause, and for the second time in his life, he felt like a nobody—empty and void. He didn't feel human any longer. What was the use in him denying that what was wrong was right and what was right was really wrong? He guessed he always gave loneliness a chance, and this was the result.

Although he was wiser and more self-confident through his exposure to suffering, it still didn't stop society from casting a stigma onto him.

This was his last cue in this tragedy. He knew Simon was something of a mystery man, seeming to be in the service of a greater master, Lucifer. This was no party; this was choice. In the beginning, he did not believe. But now that he saw the outcome with his very eyes, he had no option but to believe that the spiritual realm truly exists. It is in power. It is in control. And there are two sides, the dark and the light. He meddled with the wrong side of the spiritual. He felt like he had nothing left to do but let go of his life because not even his life was precious to him anymore. He believed that he was past the chance for salvation. And following this deception, he saluted to daylight in an array of tears, outgrown from his crusty heart, and he welcomed death in full solemnity.

SAM AND THE GANG

Six months earlier

Sam did not run. He thought he didn't need to although later it would be his regret that he didn't run away from what he had become intertwined in. He was trapped in a maze but didn't know it yet. He wanted to be known, to be a somebody. He was not one you would look at in an empty room, or on an empty planet. But an opportunity arose, and when that happened, he enjoyed the attention. So nothing else seemed as important.

This happened on a random day at his school. Everything about that day started off as normal as any other normal day was. He woke up at 6 a.m., had his breakfast, took care of his business, prepared for school, walked to school whilst going over definitions for his ecology test, and so on and so forth. He had been a consistent A student in both his chemistry and biology classes, and every other class really, except for art. His stick figures seemed more like decaying twigs, and his cat looked like a rock with whiskers. Every time any lecturer asked the class a question, Sam was always the first to respond. And his answer would keep the lecturer himself flabbergasted, not because he didn't know Sam's academic abilities, but because being as much of an introvert as he was, it seemed surprising that he spoke in class at all. At times Sam seemed like he was deaf to people speaking to him. Mind you, he was not shy, just an extreme introvert and lost in his own brain. Yet everybody made the mistake of thinking he was bashful. On one of those chemistry lessons, the discussion was drugs. And surprisingly, Sam knew a lot about it.

"OK, class, so last week we spoke about alkaloids. Can anyone please tell me briefly what these are and also give me an example? Such as Richard there ... Can you tell me?" He knew that Richard did not have the answer. He never did, like most of the other students. The four surrounding walls and the complementing desks and chairs knew their chemistry far better than most of the students before him.

"No, sir ... I forgot", said Richard, almost proudly.

"You always seem to forget. I have gotten used to that excuse now, Richard. It's about time you stopped flunking your chemistry classes. It would do you good. Samuel there ... Can you tell us please?"

He liked Samuel because he was a good student who showed respect. But he also paid a great price for it outside lessons. The bullying against Sam tended to be extreme. In fact, he usually spent his recess time at the headmaster's office. It was safer grounds there, and besides, he enjoyed his time with the headmaster as they always had the most interesting discussions. His chemistry lecturer knew that if this boy kept studying at the rate that he had been, he would go far—very far—and this pleased the lecturer's heart deeply. He had not completely failed. Sam was his little delight in his teaching career this year.

"Yes, sir. Alkaloids are a group of mildly alkaline compounds containing nitrogen, mostly of plant origin and of moderate molecular complexity. They produce various physiological effects on the body", Sam always spoke up boldly in the name of chemistry. He aspired to be a chemical engineer in the future, so this was a stroll in the park. He just understood the subject so well, like the waves understand their motion with the sea on the shore and as naturally as sunflowers turn to face the sun. To the rest, he was speaking gibberish.

"Excellent, Samuel! Can you name me an example?"

"Cocaine" was his blunt reply. He was more focused on extracting something from the lesson than on being conscious of what he was saying.

And that was when the tragedy all began. The class couldn't help bursting out with laughter. Who would ever imagine that Sam—timid, docile, naive Sam, The Nerdy Sammy—would mention an illegal drug in class? Sam couldn't understand where he went wrong. He was sure that cocaine was an alkaloid. His dad had drilled it into his head a zillion times, before Sam even knew what the word *chemistry* meant. Sam could do only what he did all his life when he was laughed at: shut up and enjoy turning into a crispy crimson, flaming lobster. Deliciously embarrassing. He hated himself for being too lenient with his word choices. He should have used the chemical name instead of laymen's terms. *Dumb one*, he thought. In the midst of immaturity, he fed them exactly what they wanted.

"Yes, Sam, you're right. Class, quiet down, please—you bunch of immature rabbits."

Yes, the lecturer hated rabbits, and that was what he called almost all his students. Some had dared to venture into the reason for his devoted hatred towards rabbits, but he never gave an answer. The truth was, he once had a bad dream about rabbits, and it kept haunting him, but he was wise not to share that little detail with anyone—no one at all.

"Is there anything else you would like to add, Sam?" the lecturer asked, just to test Sam's general knowledge.

"Well, cocaine is obtained from leaves of the coca plant, and was used medically as a local anaesthetic, although it is also widely abused as a drug. It is cocaine hydrochloride, a water-soluble salt.

It is a white dry, crystalline powder with a bitter taste", continued Sam, aware of what the rest of his answer would lead to.

"Oh, so you've tasted it! Impressive!" That was Fran. She always picked on Sam. And predictably, the class burst into hysterics again. Sam was mortified. He wanted to cry like a baby. But he daren't do so. The last time he cried, he was knocked out, almost to death. Damn bullies.

The topic of drugs always attracted the gang. And they were now fairly interested in Sam, more than before. Yes, he was a nerd, but he knew a lot about drugs—and everything, really. He had been their target for a while. Not for bullying purposes, but for darker, more sinister purposes, for a proposal, they were sure, he would not be able to resist.They could make good use of him. They knew perfectly well that Sam would be more than overwhelmed when the gang asked him to join them. They knew Sam inside out. They knew everyone inside out. They couldn't wait longer, so Jim, the leader, had a little talk with Sam after class.

"That was impressive in there, man! I never figured you'd know as much about drugs as you do! You're cool, dude! You should be one of us! We like your style. We like your intellectuality. We want you to join the gang. Whatcha say?" Jim was sly. He knew how to speak with anyone according to what he wanted to extract or achieve from them. From Sam, he wanted Sam himself. He was a piece of work, true, but he was also perfect for their needs.

"Er … er … Are you mocking me, Jim?" Sam looked at him, not sure whether this was a joke, a dream, or reality. He sometimes confused the three. Jim was intimidating, but he was not a bully.

"Of course I'm not, Sammy my boy. Whatever made you think that? C'mon, you're one of us now. You'd enjoy it with us, I promise you. Whatcha say?" And Jim smiled at Sam in such an inviting way that made it difficult to resist any requests from him. It was his charm that drew people to Jim. Otherwise, he was a sack of corruption, ready to corrode anything that breathed the same air as he did.

"O …O … OK then. Count me in!" Sam's slight stutter was more evident when he was nervous or overflowing with happiness, as he was at this time.

His innocence began to evaporate from that day on.

Sam was more than thrilled that he was about to join up with the gang. This meant he would get anything he wanted for the price of his soul. He didn't know this yet since this fact was shared only once someone actually became part of the gang, never before. But Sam thought it was quite reasonable. To him, selling his soul was only a random choice of words put together rather than reality. A perfect, flawless deal, he thought. He didn't believe in life after death, so he had nothing to worry about. He had no god, he didn't believe in spirituality. He believed in facts. And this was heavenly bliss. Nevertheless, he had to perform unruly tasks. But to him, it was worth anything just to get a piece of everything he ever wished for: acceptance and popularity.

He had never encountered a black mass before. He never believed that people actually went to these stupid things; he just thought that people bluff too much. But he didn't care. Whatever it took to get what he wanted was acceptable. He thought that they would just wear robes and sing some unfamiliar chants around a bonfire late at night in the middle of nowhere. No big deal, really, he thought. Yet deep inside he was terrified of the unknown because what crossed his mind at that precise moment was another near-death beating. Only this time it would be more difficult for him to be found. Hell, he thought, he might even die. Was he ready for this? There was no black or white in his mind anymore, but everything was the same shade of grey—confusion, misty, unclear.

But surely, he *did* die that day, just not in the same way he was perceiving. His first experience was due shortly, and in this melodramatic cue, he was to watch and learn and then participate. He read about these happenings in the papers, and on internet blogs, but he always thought they were fake, just trying to intimidate people with fear and brainwash them with angst. Karma. So he went, he watched, he learned, he participated, and he started to believe.

Then everything started to seem more confusing to him, yet somehow, clearer. But still he could not make sense of anything. What he once believed as unreal was becoming surreal, and what he once believed to be facts were now becoming senseless acts of mindlessness. What seemed supernatural became natural, and what was once natural didn't seem worth it anymore. What a transition. He was ready for it. Bring it on, he said to himself, all courageous and bold. Only two days before, Nerdy Sam had gone with the wind. And all that was left was a soulless Sam. Bring it on, he said once more to himself, looking far into the horizon, waiting for fate to take its place.

SAM AND AMY

Four months later— (two months before the funeral.)

He looked at Amy, as he pondered those innocent days when he was crushing on her. But she would never look at Nerdy Sammy and think anything else of him more than as the stuttering nerd that he was. He used to sneak a peek at her just to look at her beautiful smile.

He thought she was the most beautiful girl he had ever laid his eyes on. After the transition, he couldn't believe that Amy actually started noticing him and inviting herself around wherever Sam was going to be. In the beginning of his transition, although he was thrilled with the fact that Amy wanted him, he did not agree to go out with her. This was not his choice. As part of the transition period, he was to sleep with a number of different girls presented to him by the gang and to perform with them in front of the gang as part of the final acceptance ritual.

Once that was over, he still did not accept Amy's invitation because he was enjoying the unattached sexual company of random girls he didn't know. After a few weeks, he decided to take Amy's invitation just because curiosity got the best of him. In the beginning things seemed good, but then his mind snapped back to reality, and he saw a totally different Amy than the one he had fallen in love with.

"Hurry up, Amy, before the cops come. In this business you gotta be quick to survive." Sam had built up his confidence to such an extreme that nobody recognized him after the transition. But this new Sam brought a lot of girls to his bed, and it brought him popularity. Awesome! But this girl—there was something about this girl Amy that he loved so much. He was actually faithful towards her, and he didn't mind that at all. He was not tempted with other girls anymore because this girl drove him crazy. And he had loved every aspect of it.

"Yes, Sam, but a girl's gotta have her fun in her own way."

Amy had forgotten for a moment that once she was caught red-handed in this business, she would get a prison sentence of several years unless there was some way to bail her out. But Sam knew that bailing out Amy was out of the question when messing about in this way. Especially since the gang was in the cops' radar.

Sam cared for Amy almost as much as he cared for himself, if not more. But this time he was going to run from what he thought was true love, even if it meant running away from his girlfriend. He actually believed that Amy could be the one, the love of his life.

But love had not resided in his heart for quite a while. What he had was infatuation and lust. Maybe Amy meant more to him, but most definitely not love. Love ceased to exist within him anymore for he cast it out by his own choice, yet unknowingly because it was standard procedure of the gang, he later found out. There was a veil before his eyes, and it called itself love. Perpetual deception.

"Amy, I've told you a zillion times. Please! Anytime now we're gonna get busted. The others are already miles away. And you still want your fun!"

But Amy gave him a deaf ear and a blind eye. She loved being with Sam, but love had become as nonexistent to her as it had for him. Her home life was superficially happy, positive, and everything was fine. In their eyes she was their little darling. She was also quite attractive, so she lured the most popular guys at her school, which led her to a social life of what seemed to be cool at that moment, full of sex, drugs, and alcohol. There was never respect. So when Sam became cool, she wanted him—for his popularity, for his impressive change, but she did not respect him.

"Shit happens", she said, busy in her own little world. Because when you are on a good trip, who wants to escape it? After all, the high—the trip—was the primary escape. The psychedelic shit didn't do much for her anymore. She wanted the hard-core death sentence drugs. And she got what she asked for.

"Yeah, I'm quite aware of that. Thanks. Are you coming or what?" Sam was getting frustrated because the plan was being breached due to this ridiculous restriction called time.

"Fine! Have it your way, Sam! Go! Leave me here. I will get away with it. You'll see!"

"I hope so", Sam murmured to himself.

Amy was becoming more stubborn by the day. He loved her, but it suddenly dawned on him that he couldn't love this corrupt girl anymore, at least not in the same way that he thought he did before. The veil was coming down. He admitted to himself that it was entirely his fault that Amy became what he feared her to be. He was just playing around. Experimenting. It was never his intent to go this far. He was far more corrupt than Amy had become, and it hurt him badly to see this young and exceptionally beautiful girl turning more sour by the second. He looked at her with broken eyes, the kind of eyes Amy didn't understand anymore. He left with no goodbyes, as nothing good was going to come out of this mess anyway. He turned his back to Amy and walked towards freedom.

Sam had adopted a borderline personality since the transition. At one moment he was ecstatically in love with her, but the next moment, he wanted her dead. Sam was aware of this tempest in his mind, and he let it control him but only because he knew that it would balance itself out somehow.

As she saw him leave, she felt a pang of forlornness, as if her senses were coming back to her, but she sunk instantly as she heard the sirens approaching. She fled and hid in a shabby place nearby, thinking that when this was over, she'd leave Sam. Love is nonexistent, she confirmed to herself. She never believed much in it anyway. This was proof enough.

She did once upon a time, but then her eyes became unveiled and she could see life as it really was. She was secretly furious at her parents because they did not show her what life was really all about. They gave her only a fairytale picture. Lies, lies, lies! She believed that they preserved her life in such a perfect illusion that reality seemed unnatural. But being with Sam and the gang, she thought she had learnt life. Deceit was at bay in her, and she thought that love was a cover-up to hide the truth. She once knew the truth to be love, but now she knew it as hate. And she settled to it sourly.

He walked along the road he always walked with Amy and started reminiscing. This was over and he knew it. He was glad yet sad. She was a relatively good girl when he first met her. A hip youth—into the new stuff, but it didn't give her a bad personality. He remembered perfectly well. Her deep, soft voice had a mysterious, arousing tone to it, a tone that Sam immediately fell in love with. Her deep-set eyes lit a flame inside of him and ignited a world he was yet unaware of. He stepped onto dangerous ground, not because she was in any danger, but because the gang prohibited any such relationships unless it was based solely on a no-strings-attached sexual affair.

This was different. He knew it. They knew it. They warned him, but he was stubborn. She knew it better than he, and she became more like them than he ever had. That's why they liked her and saw her fit for sacrifice. She was unfaithful to Sam, and he had no clue about it. She was more corrupt than Sam, but Sam thought otherwise. She had done worse things than Sam, but Sam never knew because her love affair with Simon was more profound than any sexual relationship could match—not just because Simon was the best lover that ever existed, but because the force in him heightened her pleasure to different orientations and realities and because that same force brought her to a different, stronger spirituality than Sam's. And because Sam was madly in love with her, and she did not love him in return. The perfect bond.

Sam kept thinking about their first official date and how their hearts had intertwined into each other and left everyone in mystery. For it really was a mystery. Maybe Sam's soul did pay up for the emotion of love. The heart-aching music of love sounded in their ears after an array of letdowns. But fate has its own twists, and at the eye of the storm, love set eyes on sunlight. At least that was how Sam always saw it. Amy did see it mildly in this way at first, but shortly after, Simon showed her a world more exhilarating than Sam could ever show her in this lifetime or the next.

Sam's intelligence and Amy's popularity repelled each other, but Sam wasn't going to let that be the reason for lost love. Maybe he did love her. Who really knows? Besides, when he met her, he was still about to form part of the gang, and he thought that she should give him credit for that and cut the slack. And she did, thanks to Simon. It was Simon's idea, after all, to trick Sam into a love ride.

She loved the way he had started to change, his new sense of pride and self-importance. She felt that somehow her electrical love shack was starting to set off sparks in the air. God bless biology projects and preset lab couples and Simon's sly plans. Sam and Amy spent time together for educational excuses and with emotional reasons. Sam's emotions were towards her, but her emotions were driven to the rewards she would get after her accomplishment in making Sam fall in love.

When they gazed into each other's eyes and locked themselves in a deep haze of curiosity and interest, the sparks met, and from then on their love journey had begun. But the sparks in her were ignited by the same force that gave breath to Simon. But even if the twists of love had eventually converted into hate, Sam cherished those moments of innocent joy because he felt loved and believed he could love in return. And for the price of his soul, for the touch of love, it was worth everything. But he would end his life in vain, judging and condemning himself with guilt for something that never really was—dying, thinking that he corrupted her, not the other way around.

It was one massive disaster. Sam was sorry, but Amy was loving it. It was like a tsunami, destroying passion and welcoming defeat.

He regretted leaving her behind in that way. It made him look dumb and above all selfish, a characteristic that was never Sam at all.

He decided he needed to call a meeting with the gang.

"Hey guys, listen. I've got something crucial to tell you. I'm speaking with you as a friend and not as a member of the Chain of Five." This was the official name of the gang. He stopped to look at the facial expressions of the others, and they appeared to know what he was on about. "I can't do this", he mumbled, his voice shaking, but bold enough to come across as a statement.

Tears were almost rolling down his cheeks. The others sensed this, but they did not show any sign of compassion, and this humiliated Sam more than ever. But it had to be done. And even if they laughed their heads off at him, he didn't care. He couldn't accomplish the mission that was given to him. He just couldn't. They knew this; they always did. They needed him only because they knew that he would blame himself and so would society, and they would be cleared from the murder of Amy. The plan was infallible.

Jake spoke with pride."Hey, dude, this is not the way it has to be done. Be a man and stop crying. This is just stupid. What can't you do? This is the Chain of Five. You're damn lucky to be in it! Don't destroy us with your silly mentalities, Sam. Just don't."

Jake was the new leader. He used to be just like Sam—scared of everything new and dangerous. Jim had not shown up for a couple of days. He left no information with anyone, and his home address was vacant. Jim disappeared without a trace. No eyebrows were raised, though, as it was in Jim's family history to adopt the gypsy mentality, town hopping when things start to become boring. This time it was different, and only Simon knew the truth. At Jim's unannounced departure, the Chain of Five chose Jake as the new leader whilst being on the lookout for Jim's replacement, that is, the fifth member. Sam needed his first true supernatural experience, and then surely he wouldn't want to leave the Chain.

Simon was listening intently to what they were saying. *He* set up the Chain of Five, so technically it was he who owned them. They were his guinea pigs, and they thought that he ran the show. They rarely saw much of Simon as he was always claiming to be away on some business endeavour. But they knew him and they feared him and they adored him and they yearned for him, even sexually at times, for his beauty penetrated everybody he came across. He was such a strange one, yet superbly captivating. They knew he had some sort of greater force than what they used to practice in their meetings, but they never understood why he never accepted the role of leader. They always used to see him as the most ideal one for the position. But his real cue was still years from now. For now, he would lie at the side, watch, suggest, plan, play.

"Sam, you knew how I was when I first joined the Chain. Now look where I am! Leader! Courage, dude, we're by your side. All you need is more time." Yet their hearts were saying something different.

"I'm not sure." Sam was being absolutely honest with them, trusting them as fellow brothers. But their knives were already sharp and stabbing him in the back—slowly but surely.

Jake was enraged. "If you can't deal with Amy, let one of us do it. Besides, it seems to me that your relationship is far from over!"

He was secretly in love with Amy, and Amy loved Jake. She loved Simon, but she was falling for Jake. But once more, Simon's plan was on a splendid roll, and Amy was his perfect pawn. He loved this game. A part of Jake was glad that Sam called this meeting. His chance of winning Amy's heart was closer than he could have ever imagined. On the other hand, he was disappointed in his best friend. A part of him felt knot-tied at what Sam had told them. If Sam fell, his leadership would fall, and someone else would replace him. He wanted to be the one to close the Chain and have all the damned to himself. He just needed to get to Amy's soul. Simon, watching them, was being entertained. They knew nothing.

"Lay off, Jake! It's your fault our relationship didn't work out! You *prayed* for us to fail. You wanted her from the beginning! Lay off her; you can only kill her!" Sam said in a rare loud voice.

"We don't pray!" Jake replied, laughing hysterically. "Leave Amy alone. Leave her or I'll leave!", he threatened. This sobered up the team for a while. Jake thought that they still needed him.

"Chill out, dude!"

"Chill out? Is that *all* you can say? I can't deal with you guys any longer. I'm sorry."

Sam was furious. He couldn't bear the thought that Amy and Jake's relationship would work out. Besides, now their characters seemed to be much like each other's, and that hurt him even more. He turned his back on the Chain, but they all knew that he would return soon.

Jake just stood there with his sheepish look, as if he'd just satisfied his needs. Yep, his plan to be the closing leader was not as far off as he thought. He could even smell it, and he loved it. The smell of victory was at hand.

———

Gregory spoke angrily."You foolish ass, be careful with that guy! He's on the edge of breaking down and leaving us, and we won't be the ones ruling the damned, but would be amongst the damned! Would you take care of our positions while we have them please? Patience is a virtue —something you seem to lack. Don't help destroy what you have helped build!" Rick (Jim's replacement) agreed.

"Are you guys turning against me now?" Jake asked, not the least concerned.

"No, Jake, we're not. We're just making you aware that we are holding onto a thread for the Chain to survive. Blow Sam up, and the Chain collapses. Careful! Your life's at stake just like ours!"

"Yeah, you're right! Well, I'm sorry, OK? It won't happen again." His pride was humbled for a moment, but not for too long.

And the meeting was over.

The Chain of Five knew that Amy was unblemished sexually. (To the Chain, *unblemished* referred to faithfulness, not virginity— that is, faithfully obeying their needs as requested and required without hesitation.)And that was acceptable to complete that Circle of Flames for now.

But Amy was doing much more than the group knew, and in reality, they had no ultimate sacrifice to offer anymore. This was Simon's plan all along, for the perfect sacrifice was still years in the future because the unblemished perfect sacrifice had to be in actual fact a virgin. Knowing this, he still didn't tell the Chain anything. His sadistic nature was feeding off their high expectations. And he wanted to see the looks on their faces when they realized that they had nothing to offer except themselves. He did not want Jake to find another immaculate soul. Otherwise the Circle of Flames would inaugurate Jake as the prince of the Circle of Flames, and this title did not suit Jake at all. It was never his in the first place.

Simon knew that in blood, he was the prince, enthroned to be king. This was just a little fun he was having before he could obtain the power he needed. It was the title he had been waiting centuries for, appointed to him by Lucifer himself. Now it was almost at hand, and he had a plan drawn up perfectly well. It was so well designed that his father, Lucifer, laid out the foundations on which Simon was to build. Simon was the true leader. Forming the Chain of Five led to Simon having four susceptible souls by whom he could acquire more souls to satisfy the Circle of Flames. This was a higher institution of elders within the dark realm. They saw Simon as having loads of potential.

But he, too, needed to prove himself worthy of the title even though it was already appointed. With Lucifer, everything had a loophole. This was Simon's task. He let Jake and the others hope and dream. Besides, being in the Chain imposed no restrictions on dreaming. But it did make you look like a fool. It made Jake, the future Fool of Flames, look incredibly ridiculous.

Simon watched as the days drew near to offer up Amy. He had slowly and immaculately brainwashed her with her own death, and she was eager and to a certain extent even honoured that she was chosen to represent a fake purity for the Chain. She was ready to die. Simon would greet her in the next realm, and she was looking forward to a deeper love expression with him in the underworld. She had no idea what she would find there, of course.

Simon had no respect for anyone at all—least of all for the pawn. The pawn is always amongst the first to die, and he had little or no care at all for her. He did not lie when he told her he would greet her in the next life.Oh, he was very honest there, but she was not prepared for the worst horror of her life, which would lead her to an eternity with the damned. The torturous killing itself was to be her final blissful rest before the real and most painful horror was bestowed upon her.

Simon watched as the Chain prepared itself, and he was kind of surprised at how well organised they were in their work despite the underlying currents between Jake and Sam. Indeed, Sam did return because although he could not bear it, he could also not fail his very first proper mission with the Chain. After all, if it were not for the Chain, he would not be a new Sam. Now he was not sure if he actually missed being the old Sam. This new life was far too dangerous, and he was exposed to certain horrors that were unimaginable. He would have to watch through all of it, and as disturbing as it was, he did not flinch. Not even once. Even though this was Amy, he did not flinch. He watched like he was watching a movie and said nothing. He watched, thought about the past, and made his final decision. It was like he was filled with a sudden fervent approach to get it over and done with and move on to the next level. It was all about power and ranks, after all.

The sacrificing was over, and a very dead body lay wasted at the side of a road. Seeing her drenched in her own blood, Sam felt as though time stood still. An eclipse cast a shadow over his heart. Guilt, remorse, and relief!

The Chain scurried away, leaving no trace behind, waiting for their inner force appraisal. Only a few hours had passed by until they felt a conviction within themselves that they had failed as the Chain. They parted for a while, hoping that someday soon they would reunite as one.

But Sam had his own agenda for after the funeral service. His agenda or Simon's, you couldn't really tell, but it was still possibly the only sane option left for Sam to complete. He would definitely not fail that one.

PART II

An aged thrush
Frail, gaunt and small
In blast—beruffled blume
Had chosen thus to fling
His soul upon the growing gloom

Thomas Hardy, "The Darkling Thrush"

FAYE AND KAYLIKIM

A few years had gone by, and Simon stepped into his true role. After Amy, Sam was the first to die, followed by the others, ended by Jake. To Simon, this was one entertaining show. To the previous falsified Chain of Five, it was an eternal horror show.

He was the guy everyone wanted to date. He was all a girl wanted to have. He was built, had charisma, was exceptionally friendly and loveable, and his eyes literally made the girls go weak in the knees. He was Simon. *The* Simon.Popular, flirtatious, rich, everything … He was everything noone knew he was.

Other guys were jealous of him even though they secretly looked up to him. They wanted to be like him so that the girls would fall for them the same way they fell for Simon. But they always failed, no matter how hard they tried. He had something, a way to go about things, something unexplainable.

At school everyone seemed to be overexcited. The school prom was due the following weekend, and it was everyone's dream to be king and queen of the school prom. Obviously, the popular girls took it for granted that they were going to win.

"Come on, Faye, don't be such a baby. Don't miss the prom. It's gonna be massive!" argued Kaylikim.

"No, I can't. I'm sorry."

"*Faye*! Why not? Don't tell me it's coz of your sister. *Please*! It's always the same excuse all year round. You don't wanna join the cheerleading team coz it reminds you of your sister. You don't wanna join the choir coz your sister was in choir. You don't wanna join the acting club coz your sister loved acting and was very good at it. You don't wanna eat in the canteen coz your sister used to eat there. You don't go to the library coz your sister did most of her studying there. Come on, Faye! This is getting too much. It's outrageous. You have to forget your sister. I mean not *forget* her, but you shouldn't think that much of her! You have become one introverted coward!"

"Am *not*!"

"Are too! You've detached yourself from absolutely everyone! School isn't fun anymore. It just functions academically. It's got activities, fun and interesting activities, which you stubbornly shut out from your life. And from mine, too."

"I'm sorry for being such an ass. But I just can't get over it!"

"It's been nearly six filthy years now! I have experienced death in my life, too. In case you forgot, my dad died the day after my fourteenth birthday, which was two years ago, but I learnt that life goes on. The world ain't gonna stop spinning for you, girl! You should move on!"

Kaylikim portrayed a hard exoskeleton, but she was an empath, and although she seemed too direct with people, she knew how to understand them. She also knew from experience that wallowing in negativity does more harm than good. Playing the victim was unnecessary and depressing. She knew Faye could overcome anything, but she also knew Faye to doubt herself and needed a reality check every now and then. This was one of those times.

"I know, you're right, but ..." Faye was never offended by the way Kay spoke with her. If anything, she appreciated her for being that way, and because Kay was generally right, especially when it came to the matters of the heart.

"Never give up. You're too rigid for new ideas. You weren't that way when Amy was around. You used to crave fun stuff, and now you live in a dark world on your own. Haven't you gotten bored of it?"

Kay never had a problem telling things as they are. At times she had the tendency to cross the line. She hadn't quite realized that not everybody has the same grieving experiences and processes. To some, grieving comes instantly, to others, it comes much later.

"Look, Kaylikim, if you're fed up with me being the way I have become, then consider our friendship over!"

"Faye! Look at you, would you listen to yourself?"

"Whatever. See you around."

It seemed like Faye was offended, but she wasn't. In actual fact, this was one of the rawest moments she had since Amy's death. It finally dawned on her that holding on can be more painful than letting go. She didn't leave in this way out of offense, but out of the truth hurting every living cell within her body. She was internally shaken and did not know how to face it boldly. Today was her epiphany.

Faye left school early. She knew perfectly well that Kaylikim was right. Faye was sorry for the way she left her. She didn't really mean the relationship was over. They had been friends for such a long time, and Kaylikim was the only friend she could rely on and trust blindfolded. She felt a little pinch of shame arise in her, so she decided to call her up later in the evening.

"Hello?"

"Kay, its Faye."

"Hmm." Kay was offended. Having a hard exoskeleton meant she was insanely sensitive on the inside. Perhaps she was hard on Faye, but nonetheless, it hurt to watch her walk out on their friendship. Kay was the sort of person that turned a little issue into an international problem.

"Listen, I'm very sorry I treated you that way. I'm sorry, I really am, and you're right. I'm sorry." Faye was genuinely apologetic.

She loved Kay, and if it weren't for her, Faye would be a totally different person nowadays for sure.

"Don't worry, I'm used to you now. But you need help, OK? Listen, we'll talk tomorrow at school, OK? I have to go. Mum needs the phone."

Kay also was the sort of person who would not continue a phone conversation longer than necessary. She believed that many things can get miscommunicated over the phone. The traditional face-to-face encounter was best. Always.

"OK, thanks. See you tomorrow then", Faye replied, giggling, knowing very well that Kay's mum did not need the phone at all.

The next day, it was as if nothing had ever happened between the two of them. It was a sweet relationship to watch. They had the foundations of a true friendship, and although they knew this, they did take it for granted from time to time.

After lots of one-sided chatter, Faye finally agreed to go to the prom. She didn't want to ruin it for Kaylikim like she ruined all other extracurricular activities. Faye loved doing the only thing Kaylikim hated, and that was ballet dancing. Faye loved it. It was what she did to feel relaxed, at ease, and at one with the universe. It gave her strength, both physically and spiritually. And she was good at it, too. She felt the music sink in her heart, and the love flowed throughout her whole body and danced to the beat. She was a natural. It was her heaven on earth. Kay was more of a hip-hop type of dancer, but dancing was not her forte anyhow. She still went to Faye's ballet shows, even if she fell asleep halfway through.

It was finally Saturday night, the night of the school prom. Faye went over to Kaylikim's house for the finishing touches. Kaylikim was good at applying makeup and made Faye look beautiful and refreshed. In fact, it was after she made Faye up, that she decided she wanted to become a makeup artist as her life career.

And Faye was indeed very beautiful. Even when she let her sorrow mask her face, she was still as beautiful as magnolias.

Their dresses were marvellous. Faye's dress was lilac, with a few violet flowers embroidered here and there. She looked beautiful enough to make the angels sing and the devils weep. Kaylikim wore a glamorous navy blue dress that looked stunning with her Latino skin. They both looked dazzling.

Faye started to feel a slight sensation of fun and excitement in her. She hadn't felt this way for so long that she thought she was dreaming. She knew her sister was by her side, being her guardian angel. She felt her sister's happy presence, and this gave her a sense of relief and new life. At least that is what she had started to believe in order to find peace regarding Amy's death. Her past belief was based on the biblical concept that once someone is deceased, that person does not linger on this earth any longer but is either in heaven or in hell. However, she could not understand this concept. Who really could anyway?

So Faye decided that if she thought she felt Amy's presence, then she must be there, whether this was the truth or not. Amy had been queen of school prom, and secretly Faye wanted to win, too, as she wanted to revive her sister's memories of the time she won the prom. She wanted to win for Amy.

The place was already crowded, though not everyone had arrived. Everyone looked happy, and this made Faye feel a bit left out. She knew she wasn't happy, or rather, not as happy as the rest of her friends, but she planned on making the best of it—for Amy, she reminded herself. In her mind, she played the night her sister won queen, playing it and replaying it, remembering how pleased everyone at home was for her.

"Come on, Faye, look happy!" Kaylikim was filled with gladness. Her prayer was coming to pass. She thanked God in her heart, sensing that he truly was omnipresent.

SIMON, FAYE, AND THE MEMORIES

Simon rested his alluring eyes on Faye. He was amazed at the way she danced. Her body language turned him on. She was the one; he always knew it. He needed her and she was his. No matter what her heart's desires were, he was going to get her.

He was lost in his mission. While his friends were busy hitting on girls, he was drowned in the deep abyss of this thoughts. Her soul would complete the Circle of Flames. Infinity was at hand. Yes, and then he would be promoted. Oh yes, then he would acquire more power. *Power!* It sounded damn good. It tasted even better than the damnation of the damned. The mission of the Circle of Flames was finally coming to an end. The lost souls would finally become his possession. He just needed her soul—her immaculate soul of pity and pain.

His thoughts kept on rekindling like the desperate flame on a candle. As the melted wax became solid, so was the affection of hell to its little damned ones—those desperate flames that will burn up the girl with the unblemished soul. Scrumptious. He pondered on the dim flames that would start igniting her passions. The prince would gamble with her soul. *Brilliant!* he thought. He never imagined that someone like him would be granted permission to walk amongst the precious ones of God. This was hell's paradise.

"Oh my God, *Faye*! He's looking straight at you." Kaylikim had her hyperactivity button switched on.

"Who? Please don't fantasize." Faye was not in the mood for these types of jokes.

"I'm not!"

"You always are when guys are involved."

"Well anyway, he's looking. I wouldn't miss the chance if I were you. You lucky thing!"

"Lucky—humph! Who's looking anyway?"

"Only the hottest guy on the planet! Probably in the whole universe!"

"No idea …"

"You're incredible. It's Simon—*the* Simon. Ever heard of him? Tall, handsome, sexy, hot, wow, hunky, gorgeous. Well, you get the point."

"Oh, *that* guy!"

"Whoa! You're not impressed? You should be flattered!"

"Whoever said I'm not? I'm flattered at the way he's never up to any good, and yet almost all the girls are after him! I don't dig that type of guy."

"Have you lost it? Are you out of your mind? Every girl loves Simon Hun!"

"I'm a girl; I despise him."

"*Faye*! Can't you have some fun? OK, he's probably up to no good, you're right, but you shouldn't miss your chance with him. I can imagine what he's thinking of at the moment." Kaylikim had an incredibly fertile imagination.

"Oh can you?" said Faye sarcastically.

"He's probably wondering how hot you'd be in bed!"

"*Kaylikim*, you disgusting freak of nature! Please!"

"I'm just joking. Why are you so sarcastic?"

"Why are you so pathetic? It's ridiculous."

"Come on, Faye! Cheer up! You have to do some smiling around here if you want to win the Queen of the Prom title. Come, let's meet our friends."

Technically they were more of Kay's friends. Faye was just a tagalong usually, however she didn't mind their company. Sometimes they were fun.

Faye had lost that small feeling of happiness. She had a lot going through her head at the moment, and she wasn't interested in any one of the guys. These friends were at times comforting even though she had terrible mood swings and they seemed to be the fault of everything, but they understood her situation. She needed comforting and help, and they were ready to give it to her to the fullest, no matter how much she accused them. In her opinion, nobody could be better than Kaylikim, who was by far her truest friend, and had been for a very long time—since they were in the primary school. She was the one who knew practically everything about Faye, and it's due to those things that Kaylikim never broke off the strong relationship bond they managed to build with each other. They confided in each other a lot. Faye liked to keep to herself for she was too afraid to trust anyone too much. What if they die off too? She had detachment anxieties.

Zach had a huge soft spot for Faye but never said anything. Solange was the jealous one. She expected all the attention to be on her, but when all the attention fled towards Faye, she just grew further and further apart from her.

Faye's smile seemed to have faded away, and her charming, soft eyes were nearly always broken and swollen. It was obvious that she wasn't content. The reality was she was never satisfied, and pessimism took the best of her. When Solange started realizing these rapid changes in Faye, she immediately took it for granted that it was because of her jealousy that Faye had turned to this different girl. Solange was satisfied by her successes in breaking

Faye into a million nonadhesive pieces. Solange always mistakenly believed that the world revolved around her.

Solange's friendship seemed virtual to Faye, like the carpet of snow in winter. It is white and pure. But what we see is not always what we get.

Life seemed to be one virtual act. And being virtual is what Faye never ceased living up to. Faye had a tough childhood, and she tended to keep most emotions to herself. Some things she never even told Kaylikim. Home was no home at all. It was more likely to be a glimpse of hell. Faye was still the tender age of eleven when her sister Amy was brutally killed, and this damaged Faye psychologically, apart from the terrible parental relationships that went on behind closed doors.

She cast her mind, her memories, to when Amy turned sixteen and she was allowed to hang out with her friends till not later than midnight, thus adopting the title "Cinderella." She was not bothered much by this label, for Cinderella was her favourite fairytale. As long as she was happy, so was everyone else. On one of those supposed party nights, Amy never returned home. A week later, Amy's corpse was found in a black garbage bag. The sight was gruesome. Both her eyes were plucked out and her torso was opened up so widely, that her internal organs were almost all seen and scattered around. And it was noticed that her heart was missing. It wasn't much of a happily-ever-after ending for this Cinderella.

In the autopsy theatre, specialists found some peculiarities that they immediately passed on to the police. The police knew exactly what the story was like. When the pathologist sewed up Amy's chest, they looked down onto an inverted cross. It seemed that she was literally playing with fire and was burnt to death. She was sacrificed and satanically marked. She also had various scratches across her body as though she was attacked by a lion or a bear, but done delicately. They also found some tattoo markings underneath her skin that could not be seen clearly from outside. When they looked beneath her skin, they saw hieroglyphics-like markings imprinted.

They photographed everything and sent the necessary pictures to a minister who specializes in demonology.

Detective Brown had no idea how to tell this horrifying discovery to Amy's parents. The truth hurts, but they were entitled to know what happened to their daughter.

"I'm terribly sorry for your daughter's death", Detective Brown began, but tears were starting to roll down his face, too. As a professional and as a matter of policy, he was not supposed to get emotionally involved with or attached to anyone involved in his assignments, but he couldn't help it because the victim was his niece. He was advised against taking the case because Amy was family, but he assured them that being family was what made him the *most* suitable person to solve this case imminently. His determination was astounding, yet what he uncovered was beyond what he expected the details would be like. He wanted to believe that it was a mugging and drug-related murder. His hope was soon shattered.

"Apart from coming here to give my condolences, I've come here to explain to you exactly what happened. The day she was reported missing was Saturday the seventh, and apparently that was the start of the ritual sacrifice."

"Ritual sacrifice!" Al Saunders exclaimed forlornly, as if he already understood the situation.

"I'm afraid so. Our analysis has determined that Amy was killed on Friday the thirteenth. The next day was Valentine's Day, the day we found her. It seems that first her eyes were plucked out. We find this to be common in satanic rituals. It must be an utmost necessity to satanists, to prevent the victim from seeing secrets they do not want her to see. Being the sacrifice itself, she had no other privileges at all in connection with the ceremony.

"We believe that she was made to inhale a mild anaesthetic. This could not be traced. We are only speculating because certain intel affirms that some sects use it. Nitrous oxide causes feelings of mild elation when it is breathed in. That is why it is sometimes called "laughing gas". But we do not really know that she was given this or, if she was, that she did not feel anything.

"She was tied to a chair. Rope marks were on both her wrists and ankles. She was not given any food or drinks. Fasting is essential for sacrifices. It also makes raping easier. Friday the thirteenth was when she was killed in sacrifice. Because of that date, a black mass was probably held somewhere in which her chest was savagely sliced through and her heart was ruthlessly torn off from her. When the autopsy was conducted and they sewed up her chest, they looked down onto an inverted cross. We encountered a case similar to this about six years ago. In this case, Amy's heart was then wrapped up and sent to her ex-boyfriend Samuel."

"Sam?" Mrs Saunders cried out. She couldn't take it anymore. This was the worst thing that had ever happened to her. She couldn't bear it. She could picture the scene vividly, but she couldn't imagine her lovely Amy being the victim of all this horrifying murder. She thought these things happen only in movies.

"Yes, Samuel. We have interrogated him already. In fact he showed us the heart, which appeared on his doorstep on Saturday the fourteenth. He told us that whoever killed Amy was awful and horrendous. You see, that was the catch. We never told him what happened to Amy or that the heart was missing from her body. When he saw us on the doorstep, he immediately went inside and brought over the heart. He also told us that lately Amy was acting strange, especially towards him. And he thought that something bad and dark was happening to her. He tried to make her tell him the truth.

"Sam's a very understanding guy, but we still have our doubts that he is totally innocent. I definitely am not stating that he is the one who killed Amy, but there are no matching alibis as yet, though we do believe that he knew much more than he told us.

"He also told us that Amy had been seeing another guy, someone called Jake. Apparently Sam never liked Jake and tried to warn Amy that he was up to no good, but Amy never listened to him. What also confused us for a bit was that when we asked Sam why he didn't stop Amy from going out with this Jake, he said that Jake would have killed him the same way he killed his best friend Oliver. So Sam had a lot of explaining to do, and I believe he knows more of Amy's story than he told us. He warned us not to mess around with Jake and his gang."

And that seemed to have frozen time in the Saunders household. Everyone was utterly pale and speechless.

Faye had overheard the whole conversation from behind the door, and it tore her apart because she knew that she was partly guilty for her sister's death. It was not real guilt; Faye had absolutely nothing to do with the murder. But she was aware something was definitely wrong with her sister. She didn't know exactly what, but she had an idea, and she knew that if she had spoken to anyone about it, Amy would most likely be alive at the moment.

Amy and Faye had a strong bond between them. They opened up to each other often. They felt they could confide in each other in absolutely everything. In fact, Amy often told Faye about her strange feelings and her hypothesis about the gang situation. This disclosure led Faye to promise Amy that their "little" secret was buried and lost inside her heart, and no one would be able to dig it up. What Faye did *not* know was that Amy lied to her, too.

Faye was miserable. Promises are made to be broken, and she intended to break this promise, to reveal the whole truth about Amy's death. This was not breaking a trust, merely a tough fight for justice.

Faye knew exactly where Amy's diaries were, so she went and looked at the latest entries. Faye was not the busybody type and never looked through Amy's personal stuff. She knew about the diaries only because she saw Amy write in them and because Amy sometimes briefly told her what she wrote about. Faye believed she would come across something that would help Detective Brown with his investigations.

Tuesday, January 20

After school I met up with Jake. He's ever so charming. I wish Faye would see him; I'm sure she'd love him too. At school he told me that he brought me a romantic game. I was overwhelmed with curiosity. So after school, I went to his place. I told my parents that I was at Jasmine's house, studying for our math test tomorrow.

Jake lives in a deserted kinda place. It gave me the creeps, but Jake is so comforting, I soon forgot my dash of creepy feelings. His flat is quite scrappy. He lives alone, but when he entered his flat, I was surprised to see four other guys, one of which was Sam! I couldn't believe he knew Jake. But he soon left the flat. I was jumping with curiosity. What romantic games exist? I didn't know of any. And he got it. It's called a Ouija board. I have heard of such boards but never knew exactly what they are. But I definitely don't remember anyone saying it was a "romantic" game.

Jake and the others (called Gregory and Rick—Simon was also there) showed me how it is used. It works quiet differently from what I expected—like magic. And I loved it. It's like Scrabble. And scrabble had always been my favourite. I left the game at Jake's. Tomorrow I'm going over to his house again to play this original game. I can't wait! Perhaps Simon will be there, too. I still like him; he is different from Jake, for sure.

GoodniteXXxxXXxx

Wednesday, January 21

I failed hilariously in my math test. To hell with it. I never even understood the subject anyway.

I went over to Jake's again. I told my parents I was at cheerleading practice. I lied again. Jake's friends weren't there today—not even Simon. I was kind of hoping he would be there, but oh well.

We immediately started playing the game. Basically, I can ask it anything and it answers back. At one time I asked if I passed my math test. It spelt N-O … Hehe … obviously.

Then one time Jake asked the board what he and I should do after playing with the board. It spelt out S-E-X. Well, I was half surprised, since I somehow expected that one of these days we would be doing it. And we did! It was stimulating and exhilarating. I was thrilled, and I can't wait to do it again with him. It was much better than with Sam. So much better! But not better than Simon. Simon is something else.

GoodniteXXxxXXxx

Thursday, February 5

Yesterday I went over to Jake's again. I don't know if it's me, but he seems to be changing. I don't know what, but weird stuff's going on in his flat. And he made me smoke crack. I had told them I did it before, but I've really tried only lighter stuff. Anyhow, it felt good at first. But then I don't remember. I just woke up this morning on his old sofa, naked and in pain.

There wasn't any doubting to be done. I was raped. He must have mixed something with the drinks. There was no one at the flat when I woke up, but I stole some of the drugs he left on the coffee table, and I ran away from there and got home just in time for breakfast. My parents were extremely angry, and they grounded me, too. I told them I slept over at Dominique's. I don't think they really believed it, though. Well, it does go with reason. Who would sleep over at a friend's during the week?

But that was the only thought that crossed my mind. OK, I had other options, but I didn't dare tell them that while they were snoring happily in their comfy bed, I was unconscious and was being raped at the same time. They wouldn't believe me anyway. So now I'm grounded, and I wasn't even allowed to go to school. I think they know something. I hope not.

Simon called. He has been calling me lately as though he senses that things between me and Jake are kind of weird. Simon is sweet and really nice. I have been confiding in him more lately, more than in Jake. I do not know why I chose Jake over him.

Simon has been telling me some weird shit, too, like about the Chain of Five, some silly group that they form part of. He said something about the Circle of Flames, but I was getting distracted and didn't really know what he was saying.

Oh by the way, I also met Simon yesterday morning. Perhaps Jake found out and that's why he raped me? Simon was telling me about some sacrifice, but I was slightly high. I might have agreed to something. I don't know.

C ya
Xxxxx

Saturday, February 7

Jake called this morning, I told him that I got grounded and that I couldn't see him this weekend, but he insisted that it was of extreme importance that we meet today coz he has something very important to tell me. I guess I'll have to run away for one night. There seemed to be a certain tone of concerned urgency in his voice, and he said it included me. He said that it's important business.

Simon called also. Something about the Circle of Flames and some group meeting they were having. Again, when Simon speaks it's as though I understand, agree, and then forget what on earth he said. I recall him saying that tonight is the night he has been telling me about. No clue. I told him I was feeling lost, and he said that I had agreed with him about whatever is going to happen tonight. I think I agreed to pass on to a new life. Something like that. Well, I have to go for now.

Bye
Xxx

———〰〰◦⊙⟨⊙⟩◦〰〰———

And that was the last entry Faye found. She was thunderstruck. She sobbed and wept in her room. Then as though a magnetic force was pulling her, she stealthily entered the room and handed the diary to her uncle. This could solve everything, she thought.

The night arrived, and insomnia hit the whole family, except for the little boy, who had no understanding of what was going on. Once Faye managed to fall asleep, she had a dreadful dream. She heard Amy's last strident and penetrating scream of pain and terror and death—the scream which Faye held onto and never let go of. The scream that would eventually resonate with her own scream sometime later in life.

"Faye! Faye? Hello Faye? You dead?" Kaylikim was telling Faye about Simon and how good they would look together.

"Oh. Oh yeah?" She snapped back into reality, confused.

"Faye, have you been listening to a word I said?"

"Of course I have! I've been listening all along! Why?"

"You were quiet."

"I was too busy listening to you."

"You are never *that* quiet when I speak. Tell me then, what was I saying?"

"Oh, about stuff, you know, the usual stuff. You know …"

"Quite frankly I *don't* know, no. What was I saying, Faye? You weren't even listening. Why? What are you thinking of?"

"I wasn't thinking of anything. I just wandered off."

"Oh yeah, and you thought of nothing. That's absurd. I've never heard of anyone's thoughts wandering off and not thinking of anything. And look at you. You've messed up all your makeup and hair. Why are you so careless? You need a fairy godmother immediately", Kay joked, knowing that Faye got lost in the past again.

"As if … what were you saying?" Faye cleared up her voice and her act. Focus, she told herself, Focus.

"What I'm saying? I'll tell you what I'm saying. I'm saying that you should get over Amy's death coz it's messing with your life, and you need to live. You have a glamorous life ahead of you, and at the rate you're going, you're never ever gonna make anything out of it. And that's selfish of you. Faye, don't drench yourself in your own pain!"

"Look, I'm sorry. But this prom, it reminds me so much of her."

"Everything seems to remind you of her. I know it's hard. And you will never forget her. Never. But don't miss this chance with Simon. He's so hot!"

"Yeah, maybe you're right, as always. Well, I don't know. Simon doesn't seem much my type!

"I'm right! You weren't listening to what I was saying. No problem. Patience is a virtue. At least that's what they say, and I sure hope so." They giggled it off.

"I'm sorry, Kaylikim; I am."

"So will I be if you won't go up to Simon and speak with him."

But Faye wandered off again.

The prom was eventually over, and she was glad it was. She only got to say a quick hello to Simon, but that was that. Aware she sort of ruined the night for her friends, she then realised that Kay still enjoyed herself and found herself a sweet, respectable guy. They pretty much dated and were officially a couple a few weeks after the prom. These were exciting days for Kay, and Faye was more than happy for her. Kay deserved this.

In the meantime, Simon seemed to be constantly in her peripheral vision.

NEW BEGINNINGS

A lot had happened in the year after Amy's death. Maybe *too much* had happened.

After Faye turned in her sister's diary, it sure helped with the case. Sam was interrogated immediately at the police station, and he confessed that he knew more than what he had told them in his first interview. He admitted that he sort of knew how Amy was going to end up. He still had cared for Amy. So he hinted that he was involved in the Chain of Five—what they called themselves. He mentioned that both he and Jake were members but he never mentioned the Ouija board or the names of the other members, or what this Chain of Five functioned as. He kept those to himself, as that was quite an important policy, despite the interrogators having already known this. He never mentioned their intentions or their future deals. And he never mentioned that Oliver used to form part of the Chain before Jim.

Jake committed suicide a few days after he found out that Sam had also committed suicide following his second interrogation. At that time it was revealed that the gang did not really deliver the heart to Sam's door, but he somehow convinced the others that he would throw the heart into the fire himself. He exchanged it for an animal's heart at the last minute and took Amy's heart for himself.

Simon knew about this. It only made his plan easier. Sam got paid back for giving out too much information about the Chain.

Later they discovered that these so-called suicides were not really suicides. A gang law said that those who deceived the Chain or spoke about it had to face death by being killed off by another member of the Chain as discreetly but as maliciously as possible, thus making it look like suicide. Despite them not being real suicides, still, all members were eager for their lives to be over and done with. You might call it a strange version of euthanasia, performed by none other than Simon himself.

The Chain was a clever group. Well, Simon was. They never got caught. No one knew much about them, and God help them if they did. Nonetheless, they were not to be trusted, and the authorities knew that much. They spot-checked them, but Simon, being an all-seer, anticipated their every move, and they were never found guilty of anything.

The diary entries contained the most information they were able to find. Simon then disappeared.

What the Saunderses family didn't know was that the dark spirit that killed their beloved Amy was prowling in the house, waiting for the right time. It started off by destroying the sacred unity of marriage and family. Six years later, divorce was the only option for the parents.

A month after Mr and Mrs Saunders signed the divorce papers (when Faye was seventeen, a few months short of eighteen), they decided that Faye should stay in the house and live there alone. Twice every week, Jenna, the cleaner, would visit her to help her out with the housework. Faye loved this idea. It was about time she had her own space and freedom, but what surprised her the most was that her parents actually agreed to leave a house to their daughter, whom they clumsily neglected. But then again it wasn't really much of a surprise. To Faye, this meant relief. Mr Saunders moved into a posh apartment with the woman he claimed he had a good thing going on with. He promised that he'd phone at least once a week. Faye didn't really care. He neglected her when she needed him most, when the whole family needed each other's support. Amy's death should have strengthened the family bond, but instead everything seemed to have collapsed. The love that once existed in this household was now gone dry and had shrivelled up, with just a few traces of the remaining emotions of hatred.

Mrs Saunders changed back to her maiden name, Flores. She went to live with her mother and took Tom with her too.

Neighbours and others felt tremendously sorry for Faye, especially her uncle, Randall Brown. He could see Amy in Faye: her boisterous nature, yet composed, highly artistic, yet not proud; a golden heart. He just prayed and hoped that Faye would not end up in the same chalice of sacrifice her sister had.

The detective was Janice's half brother. They never got along well. He loved the kids, but he didn't enjoy the company of the parents. They never spoke about the issue or why they disliked each other.

For the first few weeks that Faye lived alone at the house, she received endless love, courage, support, and help from both her neighbours and her friends. Her uncle was a constant pillar of encouragement. These were the people who cared for her the most now. They were the ones that remembered her birthday; they were the ones she had confided in. She just hoped that this family she adopted would not fail her as her own family had. Perhaps there was something to the Christian community after all.

Living alone had its hardships. Faye had to get two part-time jobs plus go to school. She started to take ballet lessons again. This time she would be able to practice at home, in her own time and comfort, with no one nagging about how annoying it's becoming seeing her fly away here, jump up there, and swirl right here. She had her own freedom of space now, and that gladdened her heart dearly. She didn't care if she ended up with no food at times (she never really ended up in that state); all she cared about was ballet. The expenses attached to it were irrelevant. Ballet was her electric current, the means by which all her fears, emotions, and thoughts were swept away.

She tired herself out with work, and she started deteriorating at school, yet she always managed to pass her exams. Her father did remember to phone her weekly for the first three months, after which communication ceased. She never heard from her mother or Tom. She did try to contact them but never managed to get through to them. Never.

Despite this, it is healthy to note, Faye adjusted well to this disturbance, even though it hung like a black cloud. The only news she had heard of Tom and her mother was through her uncle. So much for family, she thought. She wondered if had they hated her that much. How could a family abandon their young adult just like that? No call? Nothing?

"Though my father and my mother forsake me, then the Lord will take care of me," she mumbled to herself. See? Perhaps that Sunday School was not useless after all.

Luckily for her, neighbours and friends always seemed to be around, ready to build a bridge over her deprivations, ready to give a most wanted helping hand. Even though she was humble about the fact and never outright asked for help, she still got it and appreciated it with welcoming arms. They spent so much quality time with her that she had started to wonder if they were truly doing it for her or to pay off their sins with good works. She rapidly erased that idea from her mind and stuck to the root of peace: friendship. She did deserve comfort after all.

Her week had become ultra fully scheduled, barely giving her space to breathe, to inhale the little things that make life worthwhile, and to exhale in small dozes the painful emotions that had stained her heart.

Although Faye was gradually getting over her abandonment issues, she still smelt that distant odour of deceit and evil somewhere in the depths of the darkest, furthest room away. Evil was breathing the soul of her house, and the breath was withering away her soul.

She started experiencing hallucinations and having vulgar nightmares. There was a common recurring theme: Satanism. At times, the dreams felt so real that she would wake up and recite everything in the greatest, truest detail. She blamed it all on tension and stress. She had argued against seeing a doctor. He couldn't help her; he wouldn't understand. At times she felt as if she was going mad, and got flashes of people in straitjackets receiving electric shocks. The thought terrified her so much that she decided she was not mad. A madhouse was not for her. It seemed funny, the way people tend to contradict their own conditions, but that's life, full of refutations and paradoxes.

One Sunday she was invited for lunch to the Browns'. As she stood there looking hazily at the doorbell, she noticed the freshness and warmth in the air as though the first bright notes of spring sounded in the air. She thought it was strange that just across the road, it was dense and chilly, unwelcoming and unwanted. This creeped her out, considering it matched the mood of the house lately as well as her undeniably terrifying dreams. She looked back towards her house and could not see the happy home it once had been—sort of, at least, in other peoples" eyes, it was a happy home.

As soon as her uncle, Randall, opened the door, he knew just by looking at the way she expressed her blank emotions that Faye needed to talk to someone. Perhaps they were not so blank after all. During lunch they spoke of comforting matters like how Jana, Brown's little daughter, was learning her alphabet and numbers, or how desperately she wanted a puppy and they were considering a rescue. Faye always wanted a puppy, but her dream had never come true. Her cousin's wish might ignite her own desire. She wondered, Should she get one too? Tempting indeed. They spoke of little things that made Faye forget her turmoil for a while. She decided this was a happy day.

In the meantime she was becoming close to Simon. She felt she was using him to rebound, to help her ease her pain, and by doing so, she was falling deeply and stealthily in love. She looked constantly for his company as though he was a guardian angel, able to fight away all dangers; like a knight, conquering her and wrapping her in silky safety. She felt deceptively secure in his arms.

As with any other relationship, they had their own problems. Or rather she had her insecurities. Simon was a creature corrupted in nature and thus incapable of love. He fought against love because love cast him out. So he used love to deceive. *Perfect plan*, he thought to himself. He had a project in mind, one that would lead Faye into his arms in the way he had predestined for her.

She felt like the world was going to crumble beneath her feet when he had told her that he needed to go abroad for a few weeks. He said it was some private matter he needed to attend to. He had his final preparations to conduct. Her first thoughts were that he was going to cheat.

Oh, the nature of a woman! Simon thought, laughing to himself. What a funny creature, the human. What did God like so much about them? Stupid breed, he thought bitterly.

Otherwise, Faye thought, why would he be so private? Didn't they tell absolutely everything to each other?

She was jealous.

Plan on point.

THE LITTLE GETAWAY

On the third week that Simon was abroad on his mysterious matter, Faye and her group, whom she became fairly accustomed to, decided to take a small vacation, primarily to strengthen Faye's morale with friendship and to show her that they were by her side everyday no matter what. And besides, they were in need of a good adventure.

They rented a cheap flat in a small village far from the city. They agreed to share all expenses: Kaylikim, Faye, Solange, Max, and Zach. Two weeks full of fun in a remarkable village. Just perfect, they thought.

All of them seemed boundlessly excited. They strived for adventure; it was part of their DNA—except for Faye, but she didn't mind an extra spurt of thrill and mischief. Besides, she needed to accompany her friends every now and then, even though her mind was a million miles away to where Simon was. She couldn't help thanking God for giving him to her. He was her drug, and she was addicted. Faye believed Simon was hers, but he had no boundaries. Right?

When they arrived, the villagers welcomed them with open hearts, and the visitors immediately felt at home even though Kay noticed that the smiles of these villagers seemed fake. No, not fake. Insincere. No, not even that. She couldn't decide on an adjective. They were hiding something, that much she was sure of. She could see through them like window panes. She saw the queer flicker in their eyes, and for a second she got chills up and down her spine and goose bumps all over her body. A gust of wind, or virtual reality? She wanted to believe the former, but the latter seemed so temptingly precise. Or maybe she was hallucinating.

Kay was having her menstrual period and definitely did not feel like this craziness. God help anyone who made her mad when she was on, for hell hath no fury like a woman scorned. Oh no, Kay's fury was acrid and aghast. A perfect paradox. She wanted chocolate, her bed, and her tension reliever: Bach. Oh, how she thrived on Bach's scores!

They had booked a spacious flat, more like an apartment, nothing crammed up. It had two ensuite bedrooms, one for the ladies and one for the boys. It was marvellous, just short on technology, but otherwise, just fine.

Their neighbour was Mr Baker, short and stout, just like a little teacup. That ran cruelly like a strike of lightning through Kay's mind. She couldn't keep herself from giggling.

Baker was not the delicate, fine, bone china teacup in Ms Bucket's (Bouquet's) kitchen. He was definitely not keen on keeping up appearances. (There went her silent black humour again.) He was more of a caveman teacup. Rough pottery. Haha—hilariously absurd. Say, he did look old enough to be a caveman, unshaved beard and all, right? Haha! But as they say, never judge a book by its cover. She sobered up her twisted thoughts.

They had quite a huge balcony overlooking a horizon of beauty, nature, and ... wilderness? Like a southern country movie. Or Africa. Just a landscape with character, where time crawled in mirages.

After two days of settling down at the flat and getting familiar with their new surroundings, Zach decided to go on one of his adventures. There were no DVD rental shops and nothing was on

TV. Wi-Fi connection was scarce. He was just deliberately staring into the nothing of the nothingness of this plain panoramic view before him. Besides, he didn't come here to watch TV. He came to be mischievous. And that he did.

It took less than the time that reflexes work to spot the malicious nucleus of the village. Zach thought it was some war shelter everyone stampeded into during the war. Descending stairs into a cave? Possibly correct. That's what Zach wanted to find out, anyway. He thought he could come face-to-face with an underworld of marvel and fascination, kept away from the rest of society. That last part was true enough, but the twist of fate was malignant.

He told the others about this amazing shelter he just happened to see from the balcony, and everyone seemed interested. "Seemed," for Faye felt something was terribly wrong. Kaylikim thought it was some kind of apple personification: beautifully juicy and fresh on the outside, but dead rotten and full of worms on the inside. Solange didn't want to break a fingernail, so that left the boys to all the frenzy.

Zach, the bright guy(when it comes to dumbness), decided it would be more exhilarating to explore the shelter lookalike by night—where darkness lurks and shadows go to hide in fear unless they're the shadows of the dark.

Kay shrugged that from her mind. Why was she having these thoughts again? Damn period. And it sounded suspiciously like Simon. This was getting far-fetched. She was stuck in a nightmare and couldn't wake up. Oh, the pains of being a woman.

The boys, persistent little thugs, managed to convince the girls to join them on their midnight escapade.

Every one of them thought they were up for some night time fun, but night is where everything goes wrong. They decided that before going into this unfamiliar cave (Caveman Baker the teacup—haha—Kay was on a roll in her own head—madness), Zach and Max would go and check it out early in the evening, just before dusk.

The boys, being macho men, spilt the sour milk on the floor and told Baker about their brilliant idea. He was taken aback. (Shocked, more likely.) He started stuttering and acting all strange and told them it would be best if they don't go near that place at all. But(luckily or unluckily) they forgot to mention that unimportant detail to the girls. (Frivolous boys.)But they talked it over with the girls and changed plans (for safety measures, they said).They decided that they would explore the exciting site all together on the following night.

The next morning, Zach and Max went to investigate the prohibited cave while the girls stayed at home and prepared lunch. Or they tried to, anyway.

When Zach and Max went down the stone steps, they were faced by a large (huge, humongous), black (dark, evil), rusty (oo … all gone, bad to the bone) gate, which strangely enough, was ajar.They opened it enough to pass through and descended another flight of steep stairs, but they couldn't go to the bottom. Everything was pitch dark. The sun's rays couldn't penetrate any Deeper, and they hadn't taken their torches with them, so they headed back to the flat, with nothing to tell the girls except that it was dark, black, and empty.

After lunch, they packed their bags with a good supply of batteries for the torches and food to snack on and water. At 6 p.m. the group left the flat towards their journey of fate's deadliest realities. Baker nervously watched them leave, wondering how all this would turn out. He couldn't stop praying for them for they were adolescents—the adults of the future—and they were about to dig into the unsought past. Tears started rolling down his cheek, not because he was a sensitive kind of guy, but because they were innocent bait.

He wished he could have warned them more intensely, but what would he say? That people just die in there? As if they would believe him, especially if they were pretentious kids. The village called it the Black Hole. A myth (or legend) once had it that all the unwanted evil lay dormant in the depths of the hole and erupted when the innocent trespass on their territory, whereupon they got mad, whatever "they" were. Sometimes there's more to myths than just make believe. The Black Hole was the chalice of sacrifice of evil, the veil of deceit, the field of murder, the history of the future.

Baker wished he could go after them, but it was far too late for him to follow them, so he headed back to the living room and prayed for the crack of dawn to tear up the unsolicited night to come.

Zach was first to go down, followed by Max, and then the girls. Everything seemed perfectly normal. The only difference was that the gate had been closed. Both Max and Zach knew they left it ajar, the way that they had found it. Either someone else came down after them, or—well—it just closed on its own, the way old gates screech mysteriously open and shut. Zach feared it would be locked, but the little nagging voice inside of him was really and truly scared and wished for the gate to be locked. What a lucky guy Zach was—except for this time round.

Baker couldn't keep this burden alone anymore, and felt he needed to make a call.

"Father, it's Baker. I've got some disturbing news. The new kids in the village, the five on vacation, well they've discovered the Black Hole. They're exploring it this very moment. I think they have already entered. I tried to warn them, but they're stubborn. They didn't listen. Father, it's a full moon today, and there are five of them. I fear something's going to happen to them. You need to come here at once, before the wolves start howling."

Baker was fearful. If these kids trampled on the wrong side of the cave, the Evil One would be unleashed into their village. This had never occurred in Baker's time. It was just a story that was brought down from generations before. The village was then inhabited by all-powerful Christian men and women who kept the gates of hell closed through their fervent prayer and fasting. However, times had changed, and Baker's prayers alone couldn't do much this time.

"But Baker, are you positively sure about this? You're sure they're inside?" The priest was now concerned. Would his faith be tested? Would he overcome?

"Yes, yes I am. They left at six. They haven't come yet. I saw them going down. And you know, they're also three females and two males."

"OK, Baker, I'll be there in a jiffy."

The urgency escalated. There was no time to waste. Was this bait personally called on by Lucifer? Being a coincidence, was too much to accept as truth.

"Thanks, Father, thanks."

———⟶∿∾⟶⟶∿∾⟶———

"Hmm, something's different, Max. The stairs. Er ... didn't we go down to the left this morning? Why is it that we're going down on the right now?"

"Yes, I fear you're right. Should we tell the girls?"

"No!" they whispered.

Ms Impatient Solange disturbed the guys" talk.

"Hey, anything wrong?"

White lies, white lies, and more white lies.

"Of course not. Just don't go breaking a nail. Haha."

It wasn't a convincing laugh, but it felt human enough compared to this eerie place they had decided to explore.

For a minute Kay was puzzled. Hadn't Max told them they went down to the left? "Hey Faye, why are we going down to our right? Didn't Max say it's to the left?"

Faye gave her a cynical, disturbing look. "He either doesn't know directions, or he's just trying to scare us."

They giggled. Laughter was the best medicine, right? And right now, they needed to ease up. They hadn't started exploring yet, and they were already all secretly freaked out.

"Hey guys," said Zach, "watch your steps. They tend to get slippery as we go down. They're moist or something …" But he didn't finish the sentence. Solange went tumbling down and screamed so hard that it pierced everyone's ears. But there was no echo, no reverb, like a duck's quack—like being in a vacuum. It was pitch dark, and she couldn't see where she landed. The darkness swallowed the dim light of their torches. Solange's screams stopped. And the other four were trembling in fear. She was either dead or lost somewhere.

When they eventually got to the bottom of the dangerously slippery steps, they came to a massive opening. For a minute, Zach just wished this was a nightmare and none of this mess had happened. But he was mature enough to let go of those thoughts and face reality with a stern face.

Their torches died out, so they tried to change the batteries but to no avail. Faye then remembered the candles they brought with them, so each of the four lit a candle. But there was no sign of Solange.

At the secure embrace of safety, Baker welcomed the priest into his humble place of serenity.

"Baker, this is serious. I hope you're not fooling about."

"Father, I'm telling the whole truth, although I wish it was a bizarre dream. I hope it doesn't get messy like last time. We have to put a stop to these vacations for students. They keep reviving what has been forgotten. That place needs rest. And why is it that everyone is ridiculously attracted to the Back Hole? Like it calls its prey or something. If the Evil One is unleashed …" Baker carried on reluctantly, yet he had no intention of repeating what happened centuries ago, when he was fully awakened there.

The priest looked at him, wondering where they had gone wrong. They knew the power they harboured was far superior to the one they wished would remain in hibernation. Was their faith really weakened so much?

"Solange?" they all shouted. Silence.

"Hey, come on, Solange, quit playing games with us." Silence.

They heard a faint murmur but could do nothing about it except hope they would find her alive. Zach looked at Max with guilty eyes. They were more terrified than the girls. They knew how this would end up. They just didn't want to say it out loud.

"OK," Faye said, "we'll split up and go and look for her. Max and Kay go here, and the two of us will go and check there."

"No," argued Zach stubbornly, "we have to stick together. We can't afford to lose each other. We don't know this place at all. We're staying together no matter what."

"He's right, Faye, we can't split. It's too dangerous."

"Fine, we'll stick together, but please let's hurry up. I don't like it here anymore."

So they kept walking. Suddenly, Zach heard it—a kind of ritual humming, like the *om* of the Buddhists. He dared not speak of it yet; it might have been adrenaline working hard on his imagination.

But everyone heard it. Then Max saw it, like a flickering candle in the distance. He was about to point it out to the others, but then, on the spur of the moment, the ground seemed to tremble and crumble just like an earthquake, like a lion's roar in the middle of his kingdom, the almighty roar of anger and satisfaction. The roar of truth.

Baker and the priest were irritated. It was happening again. "Baker, we have to go before it's too late."

They all looked at each other with *fear* spelled on their foreheads. "What the hell was that?" Fay asked, trembling, as if she suddenly believed she was going to be buried alive in an avalanche of rocks. But not one little rock was out of place.

The cave and the hollowness of it kept echoing in the silence. But the silence was suddenly broken by a high, shrill scream.

"Solange!" they all exclaimed, "talk to us! Where are you?"

"Where do you think you're going?" A voice slithered into what sounded like a Dolby surround system. They heard him, but couldn't see him—or it. The voice's sound was something no human voice could ever produce.

"Go *away*, trespassers! Run, you little damned ones! You have only this chance to flee."

"Wh-who are you?" stuttered Kaylikim, speaking to nothing in this nothingness. Was the bearer of this voice invisible? Was it a ghost?

"I am who I am. Do not question the unquestioned," he said in a voice that sounded like a rabid dog gnawing at every little infringement of innocence.

Abruptly, a breeze teased briskly around the girls as if giving them a warm welcome, almost suffocating them with the chilliness of its knowledge of their sins.

"Go back!" said the slithery voice, rattling his venom into every little damned one he owned.

Faye was in a waterfall of tears. They were playing Russian roulette with their lives.

"Max, Zach, lets get out of here," Faye said, shivering.

"Don't worry about light!" roared the voice with such strength that it was deceptively beautiful. They were mesmerized …No, hypnotized.

Suddenly the whole place lit up with candles, and a huge chandelier hung sneakily over their heads, like Jesus" crown of thorns—like the chandelier in an inquisitor's palace. They couldn't believe their eyes. The sight was like an oasis in the middle of the desert, like a mirage on a hot summer bypass, like a hallucination in the desert. It was awful—awful and horrendous—yet beautiful. Beautifully haunting. Hauntingly beautiful.

The voice roared like a ravenous lion, looking madly at its prey, or like a vulture hawing at a helpless little creature, picking up objects from the floor that might be edible. The vulture rested its merciless eyes of victory on the prey in front of it.

"Zach, Max, Kaylikim, Faye. Welcome. Be our guests." The voice let out a hyena's shuddering screech of delight.

There was cannibalism in this world. Pieces of corpses lay scattered about. Some pieces of limbs were freshly cut, as the blood had not yet dried up, and deep inside, they all feared that they were looking at pieces of Solange.

In the middle of this darkened ancient chamber lay a sacrifice altar. At the other side, a huge cross hung inverted. Looking closely at the cross, they saw it was covered in burnt organs that seemed to be hearts. Amy came rushing back into Faye's mind. One of those hearts must have belonged to Amy—supposedly hers, anyway. She was disgusted at this eyesore, as was everyone else. The walls were covered with all sorts of engravings.

The flames of the candles became dimmer and dimmer, and in a moment they were all blown out. They heard the voice again.

"You have disturbed my world. Now you are to suffer."

"Where's Solange?" yelled Faye.

"She's suffering the same way you will be." The candles flickered again.

Before them they saw Solange and something overshadowing her. It must have been the voice.

"Solange! Solange!"

But Solange couldn't hear them, couldn't see them.

"The ritual has begun," murmured Baker.

Zach, Max, Kay, and Faye all looked helplessly and guiltily at Solange as she was being brutally sacrificed. They couldn't stop the thing, and they couldn't go back. An external supernatural force kept them staring at Solange and her death.

Solange's eyes were plucked out viciously as she screamed in piercing pain. She sobbed and begged for mercy. But it was all for nothing;she was dealing with a heartless monster. Suddenly she was thrown to the floor, and the presence took the form of a handsome young man. He stripped Solange naked and raped her savagely several times.

The group saw that he literally tore her inside, and they realized that Solange was bleeding to death. The thing kept raping her till her last breath was suffocated by his pungency.

He then brought down a flint weapon to her chest and sliced the sign of an inverted cross in her. He pulled out her heart and burnt it in his own palms.

Amy kept coming into Faye's mind. She couldn't believe that all this had happened to her sweet, loving sister. What had she gotten herself into?

"Baker, we're in the wrong track; we're in the other dimension. We're never going to find them in time. Damn the double mirror. We came down the wrong side of the stairs."

Then they saw it, too—a flickering candle in the distance.

"Leave these innocent lives alone," yelled Father Jones at the voice. The four were surprised to see Baker and a priest coming to rescue them. Now that they saw them, they had a touch of hope.

"I repeat, leave them alone!"

"Never," the voice roared selfishly.

"Who are you?"

"You know very well, paedophile Jones."

"Tell me who you are," said the priest in a steady voice.

"*Noo!*"

The four and Baker were terrified. Baker always despised these types of rescues. They always brought shivers down his spine and goose bumps up his flesh. They were caught in what seemed to be an exorcism ritual. The problem was that this was Satan's domain. They had no right or authority here. The Evil One could be unleashed any moment. Neither Baker nor Father Jones wanted to ever experience the unleashing. Oh, the horrors that their ancestors wrote about! The village would be engulfed. Nobody was prepared. Nobody could ever be prepared for such a situation.

The candles went out.

"Let the light descend to us, oh God, oh beautiful mercy." The priest felt into his pocket for the holy host. He took it out with pride.

"Look."

"*No!*" the black shadow roared back.

"Kids, repeat after me: Oh God above."

"Oh God above," they chorused.

"Protect us with your endless love."

Zach suddenly screamed in pain. His right arm was being clawed at.

"Take this spirit to your feet. Have mercy on the souls he has eaten, and let us not fall into temptation. Amen."

As everyone finished chorusing, the voice screeched, "This is not over yet!" and laughed.

Everything fell silent and seemed safe once more.

Baker and Father Jones followed the four into their abode and decided to sleep in the same apartment with them till dawn broke free in case something might happen. They were too agitated to go to sleep. They wanted to know what they had gotten themselves into. They blamed themselves for Solange's death. The ritual was tattooed in their memories forever.

"It's called the Black Hole. It is said that to have been founded long before history began. Witches used to go to the hole to worship Satan and offer a sacrifice. Sometimes they still come out on a full moon, ready to do their worshipping.

"You tell me witches don't exist—I tell you different. I've seen them, spoken to them, and spent time with them, trying to figure out where on earth they come from. In olden times, they burnt them at the stake. In modern times, we pay them to read our destiny and perform spells.

"They seem to appear and disappear when necessary. I'm really and truly sorry about your friend's death. She sure didn't deserve such a death. Thank God we saved you four. Promise me that you won't even go in there again. Report your friend missing and keep the story to yourselves. Don't even discuss what happened between yourselves."

The priest was shaken, his faith deteriorating. He knew that only the name of Jesus Christ, the name above all names, could make the devils bow on their knees and surrender to him, the Almighty. He wondered: Why wasn't he able to even mention the name of Jesus? His tongue felt tied whenever he tried to mention his name. Was his faith that weak? And if faith is the only thing that pleases God, then is this God's wrath on him and his village? Is this his fault? He knew very well that Satan's best weapon is making mankind believe that they are guilty and leading them to believe that they are victims of everything.

The Bible speaks about overcoming. Father Jones was so confused. Scared. But not wanting to seem doubtful before the others, he kept on a poker face. How could a representative of God be scared of the powers of Satan? He had no answer.

Max said, "We do promise not to go back, but why us? Obviously, I can't imagine myself going in there again, not for the hugest jackpot on earth, never!"

Max was right, but he still managed to crack everyone up.

"So, Father," Zach said, interrupting, "how did you know where we were?"

"You will have to thank Baker for that. Zach, when you and Max went to tell him about your adventure idea, he didn't really think you would go down there, not after he gave you a strong warning that it was dangerous. But when he saw you leave all together, he phoned me up."

They felt weary and somehow relieved that they were safe. And they managed to put themselves to sleep.

In the morning Baker and Jones left the flat and left a note behind. Kay read it out loud:

> You are lucky. Very lucky. Get out of the village
> as soon as possible. Please. For your sakes and for
> the village's—Father Jones

"I don't like it," Max confessed. "They're hiding something from us. What was that hole really all about? Yesterday they said not to go to the hole again, but now they don't even want us in the village anymore. And why couldn't they have stayed till we woke up? And besides, where's Zach?"

Everything seemed to fall like a dense, suspicious cloud. Either that, or they were still too much absorbed in what had happened to them the night before.

"Maybe he read the letter and left before us!"

"Yeah, Faye, I'm sure that's exactly what he did!" mocked Max.

They decided to go to Baker's flat.

Zach couldn't go to sleep. His arm was starting to burn violently now. It was becoming dawn, and still he couldn't fall back to sleep. Baker and the priest were still snoring peacefully on the sofa. He didn't want to disturb them. They had gone out of their way to save them. They needed the rest.

Suddenly he started hearing chiming music from outside and went to take a look at what was making the mystical music, which was subconsciously putting him in a trance. He went outside on the balcony and saw a middle-aged woman, still looking exceptionally marvellous. She was dressed in purple, red, and black with gold accessories. Her hair was golden and messy. She reminded him of gypsies. Maybe she was one. She had a miniature array of bells that clanged together. She glanced erotically at Zach and called him down. To Zach, she seemed innocent and friendly.

When Zach closed the door, Baker woke up. At first he thought that the priest had left, but then he saw him there on the sofa beside him. When Baker went out to the balcony for the morning breeze, he suddenly saw Zach. He woke up Father Jones immediately. They both looked at Zach and the gypsy-like lady. The striking woman just grinned and kept chiming her bells. Zach just looked at her in awe and saw her become younger in front of his eyes.

They called to Zach to come back, but he couldn't hear them. He was lost in his own world now and could only hear the bells and exotic words coming from the luscious lips of the beauty that stood before him. The woman glanced up at Baker, and the priest and gave them a knowing grin. It dawned on them that they were too late after all. The unleashing had begun. They had no option but to follow Zach and his new companion. They realized they had underestimated the danger they were in.

The group didn't want to leave Zach behind even though he was the culprit responsible for this whole mess. They went to their flat to start packing their stuff. Then *bang!* somebody was shot down. At least that's what they thought.

Zach followed the woman to the gate. She kept smiling sensually at him. She lit the candle in the miniature chandelier that was attached to the gate. He hadn't seen that there before, had he? But it fit perfectly into the scenery.

She put the bells down by her delicate bare feet and slowly started to remove the scarf. Her eyes were dazzling, like the glistening moonlight on a bygone shore. She had angelic looks with devilish eyes. She let her hair loose into an array of beauty and passion. Her body language conveyed sexual intensity. She touched the right places in the right way, wrapping him in an embrace of sensuality.

His body was a blaze of fire, rekindling arousal and an urge for pleasure. And as he blindly filled her up with overwhelming intercourse, she called to the angel of death. She slit his throat and drank his blood as if it was fresh, running water, filling her up with satisfaction, fulfilment, and consummation.

He lay there staring at her evil eyes, feeling death linger on top of him. Innocence, what was left of it, flowed madly from his throat. He tried to breathe, to live, to take his last breath of hope.

But within temptation lies the heart of everything, killing memories, killing life.

She disappeared into thin air, and the candle blew out. Baker and the priest found him seconds later, as dead and as decomposed as a year-old corpse. Evil was feeding on every innocent inch of his body. They prayed solemnly.

On their way back to the flat, they met the others and with a nod of disappointment, they knew they lost Zach, too. There was no explanation whatsoever. Everything seemed vague and blurred and so misty, like it happened years ago, not a just few hours earlier.

If they stayed, they would have signed up the contract of the death wish. They couldn't stay there any longer. This was the chalice of death, and they didn't want to spill a drop of their blood on rotten, spoilt land.

As they left the village, they felt relief, a destroyed burden off their hearts. They looked forward to home because home is where the heart is, where safety is.

They couldn't recall what happened. Everything seemed too blurred to make sense out of anything, like they had dementia or writer's block. They had no details anymore. They were buried deep in the mazes of their hearts. They had lost Solange and Zach, and that's what they had to tell their families: Their kids were lost, ripped from life by inhumanity.

You could call it the kismet of life—what goes around comes around. But that's just a reciprocally impaired statement.

The group felt the loss of these two dear friends. With all their ups and downs, they were still friends. And now that they were gone, they really had no idea how to go about everything else. They weren't sure they didn't just leave them behind by mistake. But it came to a point: that they barely remembered them at all, as though they were preschool friends, long gone and forgotten.

THE FIREPLACE

Days passed, and questions about Zach and Solange's disappearances seemed to wane.

Meanwhile, Faye swore that the return from the vacation made her life much worse. Communication with Simon was minimal to nil, and this hurt her deeply. She had told him a number of times that she needs someone to talk to, someone closer than Kaylikim, and he had promised her he would be there for her throughout all that she goes through. But now that seemed like a lie.

He didn't phone her after the vacation to check on her and see whether she had a safe trip or if she was any better than when she left. Nothing at all. Not only did it piss her off tremendously, she feared he was cheating on her, something she dreaded all along. She had started off saying she was just going out with him, but as time passed by, her heart opened up to him, and she loved him. He said he loved her very much, too, and he said it every day. Except now he had just drifted off, like he was feeling apathetic.

To top it off like a cherry on a cake, strange things were happening in the house as though there was a poltergeist running loose. Faye felt its presence—it was evil, pure evil. And the happenings that occurred within her chamber of shelter, her home, made her feel like Simon was there. She thought it was irrational to connect Simon with all this peculiarity. Everything was suddenly so disturbing that she was feeling delirious, and she was having delusions.

But then she started to recall the times when she didn't trust him. She didn't trust her own heart and mind, and when she stumbled into her friend's trustworthiness, she gave him a try. She oversaw everything in the light to start making things right for herself, except she kept making one mistake after another. Now that she was struck with horror about the truth, she gave up on everything and everyone just like that. And she stopped being the cheerful Faye she had been so long ago.

Was this the same trap Amy got into? It seemed likely.

Although these reflections were damn close to the truth, she hesitated. She wanted a real, grown up world with her sardonic boyfriend.

There was a monsoon on Friday, and Faye wanted, needed, and desired the company of another human being in this humble home of hers(as Simon once had called it). She felt cursed to the bone. Kaylikim was her one and only option. Simon was God knows where with God knows who, and God alone knew when he would come back to her. No, she wanted to be alone. She had previously made plans for the night. Then she thought she would just invite Kay over instead, but now she just wanted to sulk alone. Half an hour later, she dialled Kaylikim's number.

"Hey, Kay, listen: I really don't feel like going out tonight. You think we can just not go? I mean, it's raining and all, and I would die to have a night in …"

"With Simon," said Kaylikim matter-of-factly.

"No. Just me, myself, and I."

"Oow, not again!"

"Not again what?"

"What happened? You used to do this when you were in your depressed mode. What did that asshole do to you?"

"Simon? He didn't do anything at all. I mean, I'm fine and all, it's just that I feel like staying at home by the fireplace feeling cosy. I haven't done that in ages, and I kind of miss it."

"Well, I won't interfere with your decisions, but even though the whole situation may sound innocent, deep inside I feel that there is something lurking. I don't know, maybe it's just me. But, now that the topic's up, I need to see you. You think you can come over here, or shall I come there?"

"Whoa, wait a sec. What happened, Kay? Why are you so concerned all of a sudden?"

"It's nothing. Well, it's something, actually, or maybe it's just me. Can I come there?"

"Yeah, OK. Just you, right?"

"Well, yeah. Why?"

"Just asking."

"OK, is eight good?"

"Yeah, sure. See ya!"

At six thirty sharp, Kaylikim was already at Faye's doorstep, soaking wet.

"Hey, Faye, it's me."

"Come on in. You're soaked! I've already put on the fireplace to warm up the house. It's getting cold, eh? By the way, perfect timing." And she smiled at Kay.

Kay had opposite time habits of most people. Most people plan a time and arrive later, but Kay always did the exact opposite. The "Kay element of surprise', she called it.

"Tell me! I'm the one who had to walk it all the way from home with a dysfunctional umbrella and all these bags. I hope I don't catch a cold!"

"Well, if you do, just send me the doctor's bill."

"Hahaha, very funny."

Faye took Kaylikim to the bathroom to dry herself off. In the meantime, Faye prepared the bed for Kay.

After settling in, Kaylikim got out a lot of junk food, a few good old movies, and her fleecy blanket.

"You seem quite hungry," said Faye, astonished at all the junk food Kay had brought with her. There was enough food to feed a whole party for a week. There were about twenty crisp packets, four huge dairy milk bars, five Milky Ways, two packs of Celebrations, a lot of two-litre Cokes, eight packets of winegums, six huge popcorns, Smarties, jelly babies, and loads of Rolos. Plus a few nachos with chilli sauce and rice crackers and lots of Jaffa Cakes and other"healthy" snacks. Binge-eating time?

"Oh my God, Kay! Are you starving or what? I'm hardly hungry and you got all of this!"

"Nah.You always say that and end up eating more than I do! But today we're seriously gonna need them."

"Really?" said Faye mockingly.

"Yeah, and did I mention that I ordered an Extra Big Mac with extra large fries and muffins from that new burger place? Delivery should be here at around eight."

"Do you want to kill me?"

"No, but we haven't done this pig-eating for a long time, and well ..."

"We did this last week! I thought you were on a diet! Plus this is not good food!"

"Are you crazy? This is delicious!"

"No, what I meant was that this is not healthy food. This is gonna kill us!"

"Don't exaggerate."

"But what happened to your diet?"

"It's a see-food diet, hun."

"Kay, summer's gonna come, and you're not going to be toned up at all!"

"I'll burn it up, don't worry. I always have. Just in case you forgot, I do badminton and fencing. By the way, next Thursday I have a badminton tournament. I hope you're gonna be there."

In no time at all, the delivery man arrived. They gobbled down everything in a jiffy, savouring every bite of it—every single crumb! They went into the living room and started off a DVD surrounded by all the snacks Kay had brought along. When they were finally seated and settled, Faye remembered that Kay had something disturbing to tell her, so she decided to make Kaylikim spill the beans.

"Kay, on the phone you said you had something important to tell me."

"Really? I did? You must be dreaming."

"*Kay*! Tell me; I know you're lying."

"You're sure you want to know?"

"Like hell I do."

"Well, I'm just telling you my opinion, OK? I don't know if it's just me or if I'm correct, but lately, well, I haven't been very comfortable when you tell me that you're going to be alone in the house. I don't know what it is. I mean, I feel a sense of disturbance inside of me that I can't really explain myself. I don't know. Even when I arrive at the doorstep, the air seems a bit denser, and it's like there's something else in here. It haunts me and it spells out danger to me, and you're my best friend and I don't want anything to happen to you."

"You're mad!" Faye started laughing. "Too many horror movies, Kay?"

"Faye, I'm serious! This house has a curse, or something inside of it holds a curse. We need to find out what and break the spell!"

"I thought you weren't much of a spiritual girl."

"Actually I am.But ... I can't explain, but the feeling is real. It brings a certain melancholy to my heart."

"Maybe it's because it's a huge house and a little me lives in it!"

"Well yeh, that, and the fact that the window to the room next to yours always seems to be lit up at night. And many passersby feel that the house is, well, not haunted exactly, but bad.Mind you, not that *you're* bad, but something in it is. Apparently it always brought about misery and death to all families who ever lived here. Call me superstitious, but I'm worried about you. You know perfectly well that your family isn't exactly what you'd call lucky."

Faye stopped to think and sighed. She wasn't imagining things was she? She was experiencing spiritual truths.

"I think you're right. Lately some weird things have been happening. I have never told you about these before because I feared that you'd laugh at me. You're right, this house does seem to be cursed, and sometimes I get frightened here all alone. And when Simon comes, I don't know, this strange density seems to evaporate, only to fall back when he leaves. I don't want to leave this house. I've got everything I possess now, and it holds valuable memories, especially of Amy."

"If I were you, I'd stop thinking about materialistic things and save myself from the turmoil and possible curse."

"Oh come on, don't cross the border.Nothing will happen to me! Besides, I've never seen a ghost or anything here."

"Don't be so sure, Faye, don't be so sure."

"Yeah, maybe you're right. But let's just say that you're right and I leave this house; where the hell am I supposed to live?"

"You know you're always welcome at our house. I already spoke to my mum and my stepdad, and they understand your position and are ready to accept you with open arms. They were the first to alert me to the danger you're subconsciously living with."

"I thank you very much, but this is so sudden. I don't know what to do."

"Leave the house and live with us."

"I don't know. I just don't know. I mean, I don't exactly know what the curse is. Let's just say *I* am the curse.If I come to your house, then your house will be cursed."

"Possibly, but I very much doubt it. I mean, no offence, but this house does look haunted."

"Well, I don't know. Looks can be deceiving, you know. I still have to think about it."

"Think well and fast."

The first movie was almost over. Amazingly, the food was half finished. Yes, Kaylikim was right, they were going to need the food badly now that they had something to feel nervous about. The tension made them hungrier by the minute. As they munched away, the fireplace became dimmer and dimmer. It was in need of more wood. Faye went to the hearth and put in more wood pieces, guessing how much would last the evening before they went to sleep.

———————⚬⚬⚬⚬⚬⚬———————

It stared her in the face, waving a blade. Her hand moved to it like it was a magnet. It looked like an eyesore with soft, delicate, innocent hands, grasping the rough handle of the beginning of a massacre. She attached herself to it without knowing why. Besides, it was an ordinary twenty-centimetre butcher's knife—perfect to kill with. These thoughts hurt her like a flesh wound. The temptation wasn't in the flesh but in anger, hate, deceit, and emotions. She was ready to kill Kaylikim. For a second, Kaylikim was a nagging nuisance, begging for her throat to be slit. She could feel her eyes turning into ... turning into what? She couldn't explain it. Her adrenaline was running way too much for her to stop this luring. Now was the time. Kay would be her first victim.

She grabbed the handle with such force that it surprised the dormant cells in her body.

Kaylikim was watching her, and to her horror she foresaw what was going to come to her. She knew her Faye. This was a possessed Faye.

Faye turned towards Kay and saw the fear in her best friend's eyes, fear that softened her up and brought her back to her senses.

She was mortified and terrified, for she immediately knew what her fate was going to commence in. She savagely threw the knife on the floor and held Kaylikim close to her warm heart, pleading for some sanity, which seemed to have evaporated from the pores of everything and everyone in the house.

By the ravenous crackling of the fireplace, the screams of the innocent were resonating in the room, trying to escape, but the flames seemed to pull them closer and closer till the screams dissolved into a high, shrill scream of torture and pain and curse.

"Did you hear that, Faye?"

Faye was still looking hard at the fireplace, trembling with fear and in shock.

"I … I … I did." Faye was thunderstruck to the core of her soul.

"What the hell was that? They sounded so much like Amy and Solange."

"Yeah, I know. Oh, my God, this is getting creepy. How do you live with the horrible sounds?"

"They never happened before!"

The fireplace was in flames, looking hungrily for souls, flickering savagely as if trying to reach out to Faye and Kaylikim, as if wanting to grab them and suffocate them in the flames and burn them to ashes. The girls were terrified.

"Who was that?" Faye was still looking hard at the fireplace as if expecting an answer to come fuming out of the flames.

"It's only me," said a man's voice.

"Don't be afraid, girls, it's just me!" When the dark, shadowy man entered the living room, the girls started screaming wildly.

"It's just me, Simon!"

"Oh, Simon! Thank God you're here! There's so much I've got to tell you."

Faye flew from the fireplace and locked her lips on his, not letting go, as if feeling secure by his gentle arms around her. Kaylikim had too much of this romanticism. Apart from feeling awfully left out, she felt scared. She wanted to cuddle up with Faye, but Simon unexpectedly appeared, and Faye had *him* to cuddle up with.

"I can't stay here for long. I was just passing by and the door was wide open, so I came in to check if anything happened, or if you needed help of some sort. I'm sorry if I scared you. I'd better go now. I've got stuff to attend to!"

"I didn't leave the door wide open though. It could have been the wind, but the wind never managed to unlock a double-bolted door!"

Well, be careful as it seems to have managed tonight. Make sure that you see to it in the morning. You never know who could have come in and hurt you." He gave her a look that she should have understood but didn't. She was at his mercy but didn't know it yet.

"Thanks, we were ever so terrified! The fireplace screamed at us! We thought we were hearing Amy and Solange's screams!"

"Don't imagine stuff! I've never heard of fireplaces screaming dead people's screams!"

"But I swear it's true!"

"You've been watching too many horror movies. My advice to you is don't watch horror movies tonight. They're playing tricks on your imagination, and you're starting to hallucinate and hear things that aren't there!"

"Simon, do you think the house is haunted?"

"Haunted? Are you the same Faye I knew before tonight? The house is perfectly fine, and there are no curses whatever here! You need a vacation!"

"I'm moving out!"

"You're *what*? Don't be so foolish! This is all psychological! Nothing's wrong with anything! Amy and Solange are both dead. Their screams cannot be revived. It's your imagination, love!"

He had raised his voice because he was angry. If she left this house now, it would change the course of his fate. He could not deal with that right now.

"But Kaylikim heard it, too."

"Well, I guess that it's true that fools don't differ."

"Gee, thanks"

"Don't worry, Faye, you'll be fine! I'd better go now coz I'm running out of time."

Faye saw him to the door, looking at him with innocent, dreamy eyes, as if she couldn't believe that this guy in front of her was hers! She gave him a quick kiss and shut the door carefully and completely.

"Faye, I'm so annoyed at you."

"Me? Why? What have I done?"

"I thought we made a deal not to tell anyone that Solange is dead! We promised to say that she's missing and we haven't heard from her, that's all."

"I didn't tell anyone, I swear."

"Then how the hell did he know Solange is dead? I'm sure she didn't go up to him one day and tell him, "Hey, I'm Solange, I'm dead"."

"No, but I promise you that I never told anything to anyone regarding Solange."

"I don't know, but things seem strange: the doors unbolting themselves, Simon knowing you're home, and what was he passing by here for?"

"Probably he was going to meet up with the gang."

"Or with a slut!"

"Kay!"

"I'm sorry, but I'm feeling insecure. We should leave the house this instant."

"But I can't seem to part from this house. My favourite place is the fireplace," said Faye nostalgically.

"Screw the bloody fireplace! You must be out of your mind! How can a screaming fireplace be your favourite piece in this whole massive house?" Kaylikim was yelling, angry, and panicky.

"I don't know. The architecture of it is impressive.It's always left a great impact on me. It's just like a magnet."

"Since when have you been into this architectural shit? We're gonna get out of here right now. I actually believe that the fireplace *is* the curse! God, what's wrong with you, Faye? You're in peril here all alone. Plus, the door seems to have been unlocked in some magical way, and I don't know how because I helped you bolt it right and tight. I can't bear the thought of leaving you here all alone. We've got to go. Screw this cursed house and come and live with me in peace and safety!"

"Calm down, Kay, and don't make such a fuss."

"Why? What reason is there *not* to make a fuss? I'm calling my mum to come and pick us up!"

"Oh come on, Kay.We'll leave in the morning, I promise."

"Promises are made to be broken. I know you well enough by now. You adjust too easily to that rule. Besides, why are you acting in this way? You're scaring the shit out of me. Why would you want to spend a whole night with a flipping screaming fireplace? Why are you so calm about this? We're leaving, and we're leaving now, irrespective of who the hell lived here and what the hell happened!"

"Fine, phone your mum."

Meanwhile, Faye was holding back her tears. It appeared she was about to be detached from her home forever. Yes, Kaylikim was definitely right, unexplainable things had been happening lately, but this house was a home. *Home:*a word that, when given some thought, gave pure pain and sorrow to Faye. This was no home; this was living hell. Now she understood.

"Mum's here.Ready?"

"I guess so."

Faye glanced one last time at this mansion that was once her home, but reality showed her that yes, this was a danger zone. Something was wrong, and she didn't know what, but she planned to find out somehow or other. She wouldn't abandon the place just like that. She'd be back, at least for the rest of her things. She hopped reluctantly in the car and never glanced back at the house.

She kept thinking about the house she called her home through all these years. Maybe Kaylikim was acting as the third wheel and set up props to scare her out of the house and out of Simon's life. But she never mentioned Simon, right? And it wasn't as if Kay told her to become homicidal.

Maybe she should tell all of this to Simon. Except he was acting rather strange lately. And how did he manage to open the door without the alarm ringing? She wondered whether Simon was the culprit behind all of this. And from wonder, it became belief. And just as if he was reading her mind, Simon called her on her cell phone.

"Hey, Faye, where are you? I came over to your place and you're not here."

"No, I'm not, Simon. I'm on my way to Kaylikim's. I'm gonna be spending the night there. Weren't you there like two hours ago?"

"Yeah, but I thought I'd surprise you and come back, you know, for a special night."

"Oh how very thoughtful of you. Well I'm sorry, Simon, but I have to go. Besides, my battery is almost out, so don't bother trying to call me."

And she hung up the phone.

Kay looked at her in surprise. Faye was always overjoyed when Simon called, and now all of a sudden she didn't even want to speak to him.

"Faye, are you OK?"

She just nodded in agreement, and let her eyes fill up with tears. Let the waterworks begin.

She knows, thought Simon. But how, he didn't know. He heard her through her voice. She knew he was the guilty party behind this mess. But he'd fix it. Besides, her time was up. The angel of death was due to visit her very soon. Oh, his smile started to stretch. Soon he'd reign over the Circle of Flames. Finally … finally.

Kaylikim hated watching Faye drown in desperation like she had uncovered the past to rewrite the future, but she couldn't do that. It was just a little absurd thought that still made sense for a second.

Faye just wished she had had a better life, a better everything. Everyone said she was lucky, but she never felt that way. On the contrary, she felt cursed to the core. And now she knew that the curse was at its end. She felt relieved yet sad. All the little things that mattered in life she had taken for granted. And now, at her bitter end, she needed that last comforting hug, that last miracle Of a rainbow, that last beauty of nature acting at its perfection.

Faye was blessed with beauty and talent, but those never really mattered. They didn't buy love, education, a home. They bought turmoil and misery.

A few days later, she decided to go for a walk in the country. Snow had accumulated and it was beautiful—so pure, so perfect, so innocent. Wandering about, enjoying that last fresh breath of air, Simon became present.

And with a knowing glance, she let him take her over; there was no use in fighting anyway. She was secretly praying, not that it wouldn't hurt, but that she would be the last victim. During her time at Kaylikim's, she immersed her thoughts in everything that had happened since Amy's death, and it all had started making sense to her. She realized that her time was up. Simon sent her subtle signs all along. He sent her a dream, too, that explained everything that had to come to pass. She had to accept it. Otherwise it would haunt her for the rest of her life and also the seeds she produced along with their generations. She surely didn't want that.

As she walked her last parade on an icy boulevard of frozen emotions, her mind wandered to his body of fire and his heart of ice. Oh, she knew her fate now. This was his game. She was his fragile pawn, deceived to the brittle bone, corroded by disbelief.

He was thirsty, anxious to suck out all her pure blood in the most painful and unbearable way. He was greedily anxious to establish his own reign. After hundreds of years, he started to feel success sink in. Although he had been created, like energy, he could neither be recreated nor destroyed, only transformed into different levels of evil.His last configuration would sum up his eternal power.

This path of realization brought her to actuality. On this inauspicious day, she learned that appearances do not lead to the truth. The seeds of hatred had been sown well. Even Satan can come as an angel of light, and my oh my, Simon was the most beautiful angel she had ever seen. She understood the full extent of her own folly and had to pay a heavy penalty for all her mistakes.

Whilst walking towards her death throne, Faye realized that every puzzle has its pieces. She had faith that reality teaches that the good does not outlast the bad. But why have faith when there's no fate?

Simon breathed life out of Faye, the same sweet breath that excited her. The mist was so thick that a knife would be needed to slice through it—the same way he sliced through her.

Only he slashed through her savagely and blended into the icy, misty air as if he was a ghost.But he wasn't, was he? She was left there alone, trying to defeat death, but the blasts of winter swept her cold life away. The last crackling flame stopped flickering, and Simon was due to attend his coronation.

PART III

A snowflake is one of God's most fragile creations, but
look what they can do when they stick together.
Anonymous

KAYLIKIM, GRIEF, AND VICTORY

The blizzards blew on end; everything was pale, wet and uncomfortable. Warm thoughts passed through her head of rainbows and butterflies and velvet kisses. But nothing could Ease the eyesore before her. The cherry blossom trees were glazed, shielded from the old cruel world, just like the thoughts that ran through her head. Her fingers were numb, and the wind was howling at such a high volume that she felt she was temporarily going deaf.

Faye lay motionless on the soft, peaceful snow. It looked like a perfect match. Kaylikim tried to cry, but no tears came out. The shock was too great for her to make any form of facial expression. She saw the blood carelessly splattered on the snow, soaked in patches of pain.

She closed her eyes, hoping this was one bad nightmare that would vanish the second she opened them. Again she thought of pleasant things but to no avail. Before her lay the body of an immaculate young lady, Faye, the only true friend she had ever had.

She knelt down beside her and smiled at her radiantly pallid face. She kissed her on the cheek and would have sworn that for a second Faye smiled back. Kaylikim stood up, said a little prayer of sorrow, turned around, and walked away from the heavy weight of emotional pain and suffering. She glanced behind her, saw her footsteps in the snow, and thought about how Faye had left permanent footsteps in her heart—a trail that would forevermore be hollow.

She arrived home, lay on the sofa, and slept for what seemed like hours. She dreamt of a perfect world of blue roses, blossoming trees, and fairytales. She was wandering in a world of pure bliss, and the sky was raining colours as the sun strengthened the warmth in her heart. Butterflies whispered songs of unimaginable beauty, and rainbows were kissing her peachy soft skin.

Then everything went black. The earth shook with anger and screamed out of disappointment. The sun was drowned and the stars cried balls of fury and misery. The land grew dark, moist, and unbearably cold. The earth spit blood in ravenous rage. Shadows of darkness suffocated her last visions till she woke up gasping for air. She heard sirens outside her house and knew this was not good news. Her vision was still blurred, and someone was calling out her name from a distance. There was a tone of both panic and relief. Something was on her face. She could make out the shape of a mask. Breathing hurt a bit, and everything pointed towards an understanding of confusion.

She moved her limbs slightly, but they felt heavy. When she tried to turn her neck, it hurt her badly. A strange thought crossed her mind that perhaps somehow she was strangled or tried her luck at suicide.Nonetheless, she knew that she just drifted off into her perplexing dream. Her vision was getting clearer, and breathing seemed less of a hassle.The voices weren't distant anymore, and everything seemed to come back to normal. She saw paramedics surrounding her.They asked her to take deep, long breaths, but she was curious. She tried to speak, but no words formed. She tried to mumble something, but noises too were utterly useless. She fought with her innerself and finally managed a weak croak. Her mother hushed her. Paramedics kept making her do things that seemed harder than impossible. Her mother spoke in a comforting tone yet was tearful and on the verge of breaking into hysterics.

"Baby, relax. Just please stay with us; please don't leave me."

Then her vision started getting blurry again and she began to feel nauseous. She let her body go lose, and she drifted back to her vivid dream with her mother's tormented echo of three urgent words: I love you.

Once more she saw herself in a world of mystery. But this time she knew she wasn't alone.

She saw the faces of the people she had lost: her dad, Amy, Solange, Zach, and Faye. The beautiful face of Faye—all their faces were stern, and looked as though they were in pain. Was this hell? Were they in hell? How could it be? And was she dead and in hell, too? There was no lake of fire, though.

Kay called out Faye's name, but Faye could not speak. She tried to open her mouth, but it seemed forced shut. She could only whimper inside. She was scared. The Bible does say that hell is filled with weeping and gnashing of teeth, but surely it did not mention the true horrendous things that take place there. Kay realised that hell's starting point was from earth. Was this a vision or a dream? She couldn't decipher it.

She started coming back to her senses and stabilising herself.

"Oh my baby!" cried her mother. "How do you feel?"

"Tired," said Kay. "What happened?"

"You don't remember?"

"Well, I had a nap on the sofa, and here I am."

"Kay, you have been in a coma for two days!"

"So why am I not in hospital?"

"Good question. When the paramedics tried to move you, you fought them off forcefully …somehow. I can't explain it, and neither can they. So they recommended keeping you here with two of them observing you continuously. And now you are awake.

Can we take you to hospital for further tests? Or is that going to be a problem again?"

"Mum, I don't know what you are talking about, but if I need to go, then obviously I'm going!" Kay still thought this all made no sense at all.

She spent a further three days in hospital for testing and observations, but all results came back normal. There was no explanation for Kay's strange coma.

However Kay, knew it to be a blessing. During the time she spent in hospital, she immersed herself in the Word and realized that she could end the curse that stole Faye's life, and which, according to her dream, was after her own life, too.

She had always believed in God, and her mother and stepfather were devoted Christians. Kay didn't read the Bible much, but her faith was in none other than Christ himself. She read parts of the Bible, and it dawned to her what power this book really has—a power known only to those who are truly followers. This book has the power to stop the plans of Satan—and she was about to do just that. She was the flaw in Simon's plan. Simon knew this, and that's why he took murderous possession of Faye on her last night at her house.

Once she was out of the hospital, she went back to that village the group had visited to meet up with Baker and Father Jones. She went, but the whole town was desolate and abandoned. A fire seemed to have burnt down most everything. The land was barren. Could this have been the work of the"unleashing', whatever it was? She headed back home, not knowing what really happened there. Did they die? Did they flee? She would never know that.

She arrived back home, went to her room, and took a nap. She slept profoundly, and then the oddest, most horrendous thing came upon her:She experienced sleep paralysis. Her eyes were wide open, and she could see this monstrosity holding her down, putting a load of weight upon her chest and strangling her with cruel fingers. As she looked into the emotionless eyes of this creature, she tried to make a sound, but her tongue was tied down, too. She tried with all her strength to move her limbs but couldn't even twitch. In the corner of her room, she saw Simon—smiling, then laughing, then drawing close to her. Kay was losing her breath. She didn't want this to be her ending. She didn't want Simon's face to be the last she sees.

"So you thought you could defeat me just because you started to read the Bible?" he said and laughed at her.

Loud and proud, Simon proclaimed: "It's just an old book. There is no truth in there. It's just a bunch of fairytales. Everyone's fate is the same. Everyone goes to hell. There is one God, and he is Lucifer."

His words were not weakening the faith of Kaylikim.If anything, they were strengthening it further! She tried to shake her head in disagreement, but this creature above her kept strangling her and immobilizing her.

"Kay, you can't move. I have cast this presence to suffocate you to death whilst I recite to you who and what the truth really is."

Kay was paralyzed in body, but her mind could still think. She went through the verses she had read from the Bible to try and find the key to defeating these monsters. She knew that it was in the name of Jesus, but how could she proclaim that when her own voice was silenced by the enemy?

"You can find nothing in the Bible that will help you release yourself from this," Simon assured her. But as with everything, there was a loophole for such a situation, and Kay was not about to relent until she found it.

"It brings me joy to see you in this way. I have been crowned already. All your efforts are useless now."

Kay realized that Simon was not that beautiful man she knew. He barely even looked like a human being and definitely not like a beautiful angel. This was his truth.

Then, the powerful book revived a thought in her. There was after all one thing that could make her victorious over this. She rested, knowing very well that her fate was really sealed in Jesus and not in Simon's master.

She accepted the unleashing of spiritual tongues within her and started forcing them through her mouth till her tongue had to surrender to the one true master. This language was the only thing Satan and his followers could not understand, the only language that directly connects a person to God. This was her only chance.

Once she gained control over herself and saw the creature upon her vanish, she saw Simon as the demon he truly was.

She had power within her that she had never felt before. And in that moment, she knew that it was the power of God within her that led her to cast Simon to his well-deserved place. She crushed the curse from her life, from her being, from her family, from her home, from her future.

"In the name of Jesus Christ", she shouted at Simon whilst he screamed in agony and disbelief that he had lost it all.

"In the name of Jesus Christ", she repeated, terrifying Simon's core essence.

"In the name of Jesus Christ", she affirmed, vanquishing Simon from the realm of time.

"In the name of Jesus Christ" she cried, weeping with joy at the realisation that no power formed against her could ever prosper!

Put on the whole armour of God that you may be able to stand against the wiles of the devil. For we do not wrestle against flesh and blood, but against principalities, against powers, against the rulers of the darkness of this age, against spiritual hosts of wickedness in the heavenly places.—Ephesians 6:11, 12

ABOUT THE BOOK

It all started centuries ago when the fallen Lucifer appointed Simon to form the Chain of Five. At completion, he would earn a high status in the realm of darkness. He has to kill Amy to get to Faye—his final chosen sacrifice, only to find out that there was a flaw in his plans that would ultimately turn the tables on the dark forces and on his position.